ROBOT WARS

ROBOT WARS

SIGMUND BROUWER

BOOK TWO

DOUBLE CROSS

TYNDALE HOUSE PUBLISHERS, INC.
CAROL STREAM, ILLINOIS

You can contact Sigmund Brouwer through his Web site at
www.coolreading.com or www.whomadethemoon.com.

Visit Tyndale's exciting Web site for kids at www.tyndale.com/kids.

TYNDALE and Tyndale's quill logo are registered trademarks of Tyndale
House Publishers, Inc.

Double Cross

Previously published as Mars Diaries *Mission 3: Time Bomb* and Mars
Diaries *Mission 4: Hammerhead* under ISBNs 0-8423-4306-7 and
0-8423-4307-5.

Double Cross first published in 2009.

Designed by Mark Anthony Lane II

For manufacturing information regarding this product, please call
1-800-323-9400.

Library of Congress Cataloging-in-Publication Data

Brouwer, Sigmund, date.
    Double cross / Sigmund Brouwer.
        p. cm. — (Robot wars)
    This edition combines the contents of Mars diaries, Mission 3, Time bomb
and Mars diaries, Mission 4, Hammerhead under title Double cross.
    Previously published in 2 vols.
    ISBN 978-1-4143-2310-7 (softcover)
    I. Title.
    PZ7.B79984Dm 2009
    [Fic]—dc22   2008034381

Printed in the United States of America

15   14   13   12   11   10   09
8   7   6   5   4   3   2

THIS SERIES IS DEDICATED
IN MEMORY OF MARTYN GODFREY.

Martyn, you wrote books that reached all of us kids at heart. You wrote them because you really cared. We all miss you.

FROM THE AUTHOR

We live in amazing times! When I first began writing these
Mars journals, not even 40 years after our technology allowed
us to put men on the moon, the concept of robot control was
strictly something I daydreamed about when readers first
met Tyce. Since then, science fiction has been science fact.
Successful experiments have now been performed on monkeys
who are able to use their brains to control robots halfway
around the world!

Suddenly it's not so far-fetched to believe that these
adventures could happen for Tyce. Or for you. Or for your
children.

With that in mind, I hope you enjoy stepping into a
future that could really happen. . . .

Sigmund Brouwer

JOURNAL
ONE

CHAPTER 1

On the side of the cliff, I hung from a thin metal cable.
Hundreds of feet below, the jagged red rocks of the Martian
valley floor pointed up at me like deadly spears.

The temperature had risen from minus 100 degrees
Fahrenheit to a nice, warm minus 20 degrees Fahrenheit.
Wind pushed at my body, making me sway from side to
side. But it could have been worse. I could have been stuck
in a sandstorm, with grains of sand hitting me at 60 miles
an hour, rattling off my titanium shell and blinding me
completely.

As it was, I had a good view. On Mars at midday, when
the sand isn't blowing, the sun is blue against a butterscotch-
colored sky. The clouds are barely more than stretched-out
strings of fog, lighter blue than the sun.

I could look across the entire valley and see the oranges and reds of Martian soil. Nearly 10 miles away, a gigantic dome held all 200 of the scientists and techies who founded the first colony on Mars. Under that dome were oxygen and water and warmth and food, all the things humans need to survive.

Out here? There was no oxygen. No water. No warmth. And no food. My robot body didn't need any of that.

Of course, those jagged rocks waited for any mistakes. From where I was, it wouldn't matter much that gravity on Mars is about a third of Earth's gravity. If my grip on the cable slipped, those rocks would tear through my robot body like daggers. What made it worse was that I had a passenger strapped to my back.

My job was to make it to the bottom of the cliff with both of us undamaged.

At the top, the metal cable was attached to a long spike driven deep into the soil. All 300 feet of the cable dangled from this spike.

I held on to the cable with a gripper in each hand. Each gripper clamped the cable securely with much more power than I could have gotten by using just my fingers.

The trick was to unclamp the gripper in my right hand and hold on with the gripper in my left hand. Then I had to bring my free right hand down and reclamp at a level below my left hand. Once the right-hand grip was secure,

I unclamped the left and reclamped it below the right. And so on. It was slow work that took a lot of concentration.

One thing made this easier. My lower body was on wheels, so all I had to do was let myself roll down the cliff. Slowly. Very slowly.

I was halfway down when it happened.

As I leaned against the cliff, my right wheel hit a loose portion of rock. It broke away, clattering down the cliff. My right side swung inward, spinning me sideways. This wouldn't have been a problem if I'd been clamping the cable with both grippers. But I was holding with only my left.

In panic, I grabbed at the cable with my right hand. Because I was spinning, I missed the cable and jammed my hand into the cliff. This pushed me away from the cliff too hard. For a second, I was like a pendulum. With less gravity on Mars than on Earth, my action shot me six feet away from the side of the cliff and then banged me against rock on the return.

It felt like I'd been slammed with a baseball bat. Keeping my grip on the cable with my left hand, I fought to find the cable with my right. But I was off balance. Especially with a passenger on my back. My wheels began to roll upward on the cliff wall as the weight on my back pulled me upside down and backward.

The cable twisted more. Still I tried to find a grip with my right hand.

Nothing.

Then . . .

Snap. The buckle keeping the passenger on my back opened, and suddenly I had no passenger.

"Rawling!" I shouted as I watched the downward tumble of arms and legs. "Rawling!"

Seconds later, there was an explosion of dust as the body smashed into the rocks.

I had failed my mission.

CHAPTER 2

I woke up blindfolded and on my back on a narrow medical bed in the computer laboratory.

"Rawling!" I called again. It had taken nearly half an hour to climb to the bottom of the cliff. And another 20 minutes to get back to the dome. Then a few minutes to get inside and park Bruce, the robot body, where it needed to be charged. "Rawling!"

Here in the lab I wore a headset too, so I couldn't hear anything, not even my own voice as I shouted. My arms and legs were strapped to the bed so I couldn't move. I was help-less until Rawling McTigre reached me. He was a doctor and a scientist who worked with me on my virtual-reality missions.

It took a few seconds. He lifted the blindfold, and I blinked against the lights. Next came my headset. We did all of this because it was important that nothing distracted my mind from operating the robot body.

"Thanks," I said, glad I could see and hear through my own eyes and ears now. Not being able to do that was one of the things I didn't like about being hooked up through virtual reality to a robot. But the advantages were great, especially to a kid who was unable to use his legs. Something had gone wrong during an operation on my spine when I was too young to remember, so now I was in a wheelchair. Yet because of that and a computer link in my spine, I was the only one who could explore the planet of Mars in a robot's body.

"You all right, Tyce?" Rawling asked, concern on his face. "The signal was clear, and I got a video feed of everything that happened."

"I'm all right," I said. "But I'm afraid if this hadn't been a test run, someone on Bruce's back would be very dead right now. That crash-test dummy you rigged really did become a crash test."

When the robot body had rolled to the base of the cliff, I'd found the dummy. It was—or had been—the weight of a human. But in the fall, the legs and arms had ripped off, and the jagged rocks had speared the body portion. I shuddered to think of what those rocks would have done to a real person.

"Mistakes are not always a bad thing," Rawling said as he unstrapped me and helped me sit up. "From what I can tell, the dummy was positioned too high. We need to strap it lower, closer to the center of gravity."

"One other thing," I said.

Rawling arched an eyebrow, the way he always did when he wanted to ask a question. He'd been a quarterback for a university back on Earth when he was younger, and his wide shoulders showed it. Now his short, dark hair was streaked with gray. One of two medical doctors under the dome, he'd also recently been appointed replacement director of the Mars Project. It might sound strange to say that though he was in his mid-40s and I was only 14 (in Earth years), Rawling was a great friend. After all, until a month ago I'd been the only kid under the dome, so I didn't expect friends my age. Also, Rawling had worked with me for hours every day since I was eight, training me in a virtual-reality program to control a robot body as if it were my own.

"You don't need to worry about the strap," I continued. "That's not why the dummy fell away from me."

He arched his eyebrow again.

"It's the buckle," I said. I pictured how it had opened. "While I was swinging, it banged into a piece of rock. That's what released it. You need some sort of safety guard on it."

"Good point," Rawling said. "Very good point. I'll get one of the techies to make the changes right away."

What was his rush? I wondered. Today was supposed to

be a normal school day for me, and Rawling had asked me to take time off to learn cliff climbing. "Rawling?"

"Yes?" He lifted my legs off the bed and helped me into my nearby wheelchair.

"Why are we doing this?" I asked. "I mean, you don't expect that someday I'll actually have to lug someone down a cliff?"

Rawling didn't answer. Instead, he walked over to the computer and the transmitter and began to shut down the power.

"Rawling?"

He finally turned to me. "Tyce Sanders," he said in a strange tone, "meet me in my office in five minutes."

CHAPTER 3

Until recently, the director's office had belonged to someone else. In the month since Rawling had taken over as director, he'd been so busy that he hadn't made any changes yet. The framed paintings of Earth scenes, like sunsets and mountains, still hung on the walls. Blaine Steven, the former director, had spent a lot of the government's money to get those luxuries included in the cargo shipped to Mars. But even a director didn't get bookshelves and real books. Cargo was too expensive. If people wanted books, they read them on DVD-gigarom.

Usually I admired the framed paintings because no one else in the dome had them. This time, however, my attention was on Rawling.

"Tyce," Rawling said from behind his desk, "I don't want to believe what I think I'm seeing."

"You're seeing me," I said with a grin. He seemed so serious that I wanted to lighten him up. "What's hard to believe about that? You called for me five minutes ago, and here I am."

"Very funny," he said. No grin. "Let me get you a microphone and a crowd so they can throw tomatoes at you."

"Tomatoes?"

As the only human ever born on Mars, I'd never been to Earth. But I knew tomatoes were something people on Earth grew and ate. I'd seen photos of them on my digital encyclopedia, but I'd never tasted them. And I sure couldn't figure out why people would throw them at me.

"It's an old Earth thing," Rawling explained, obviously wishing he hadn't started this. "When they don't like a comedian or an actor, they throw rotten vegetables at him."

"Hmm," I said. "You sure tomatoes are vegetables? Some people argue that—"

"Not now. Please, not now." Rawling stood and walked around his desk to where I sat in my wheelchair. "These are digital photos from the satellite," he said, waving sheets of paper at me. Rawling meant the communications satellite that circled Mars. "If I'm seeing what I believe I'm seeing, you've got to promise to keep this absolutely secret. I'll be making a public report as soon as possible, but until then . . ." He handed the photographs to me.

I studied them. Mars has nearly zero cloud cover, so unless a gigantic sandstorm is brewing, the satellite takes very clear photographs. They are sent by radio transmission to a computer here under the dome, then digitally translated into printouts of photos of the planet's surface.

What I saw in the photographs were different shots of a valley. In real life, the soil would be red and brown and orange. The black-and-white digital printouts just showed different shades of gray. The satellite had provided long shots and close-up shots, all taken from directly overhead, some five miles above the surface of the planet.

"Wow," I said. "Rocks and more rocks. This looks so scary I don't think my heart can take it."

Rawling sighed and squatted beside my wheelchair. "That," he said, pointing to a square black rock in the center of one of the close-up photos, "is what's truly scary."

Sensing he'd had enough of my joking around, I didn't make any more dumb remarks.

"Notice how absolutely smooth and square that rock is," Rawling said.

Now that he mentioned it, I could see it was.

"You can't tell from the photo, but it's about the size of this office," he continued. "Now keep looking. You'll see several more."

He was right. In the jumble of boulders in the valley, I counted four more of those strangely smooth, strangely square gigantic rocks. "You've got me interested," I said. "What are they? How did they get there?"

"Not so fast," Rawling said firmly. He paced for a few seconds, then stopped. "First question: why haven't we seen them before? I mean, our satellite has been circling Mars ever since the dome was established almost 15 Earth years ago. Suddenly this."

I thought of yesterday's big event. A rumble had shaken the dome. It felt like an earthquake—marsquake—had occurred miles and miles away. Or like an asteroid had banged into Mars. Although no damage had been done, it had rattled things briefly, and it was all anyone could talk about— scientists in their labs, techies running the experiments for the scientists, me, Mom, Dad, and my new friend, Ashley Jordan.

"First answer," I guessed. "It has something to do with that explosion we felt yesterday."

"Exactly. There's a lot of soil now exposed to the surface that wasn't there before yesterday. In other words, those square black things were buried."

"I give up," I said. "What are they? How did they get there?"

Rawling shook his head. "All I can tell you is I'm nearly certain those black things aren't a natural part of Mars."

"They couldn't have come from Earth," I reasoned. "Otherwise we'd know about them already, right? I mean, the Mars Project is the first time anyone from Earth has landed on Mars. And if no one from Earth put them there . . ." I stopped, too afraid to say what I was thinking: *If no one from Earth had put them there, who had done it?*

Rawling read my mind. He nodded. "Now you understand why I don't want to believe what I think I'm seeing."

"Now I understand," I answered.

"Which is why I called you here," he said slowly as if he wished he hadn't had to call me into his office.

"Yes?" I asked.

"Tyce, you can say no if you don't want to do it."

"No to what?"

"It's absolutely *imperative* that we take a closer look at those things. The trouble is, it won't be as easy as a practice run. Not considering where we need to go."

That's when Rawling went over his plan with me, step by step.

CHAPTER 4

"Why is there something instead of nothing?" Ashley asked me, hand on her right hip in her trademark pose.

I'd promised Rawling I'd return to work with him after talking through his plan with my mom, Kristy, a leading plant biologist, and my dad, Chase, an interplanetary pilot. But first I'd wheeled across half of the dome to return to where Ashley and I had been studying some math questions.

Since the dome's total area was about the size of four Earth football fields, I never had to travel far. Besides the small, plastic minidomes of the scientists and techies, there were experimental labs and open areas where equipment was maintained. The main level of the dome held the minidomes and laboratories. One level up, a walkway about 10 feet wide circled the inside of the dome walls. People mostly used the walkway for jogging. Not me, of course. The techies had built a ramp for my wheelchair so I could access the second level and then the third and smallest level by a narrow catwalk.

Centered at the top of the dome, this third level was only 15 feet wide. On its deck a powerful telescope perched beneath a round bubble of clear glass that stuck up from the black glass that formed the rest of the dome. From there, the massive telescope gave an incredible view of the solar system.

This was my home, and I loved it. And it was even better now that I had a friend my age. A month ago Ashley Jordan had arrived on the most recent spaceship with her father, Dr. Shane Jordan, a quantum physicist. Like me, she was a science freak. Even better, she was fun to be around—even if she did ask strange questions. *Something instead of nothing?*

"Something what?" I asked. "Nothing where? I thought we were going to work on calculus."

It was midafternoon. We sat in an open area near the gardens, with the giant curved ceiling of the dome stretching in all directions. It was quiet here, with only the occasional conversations of passing scientists or techies to interrupt us.

"Calculus." Ashley made a face, as if she'd tasted something awful. "More fun to daydream." Pointing to her handheld computer, she continued, "And I was getting tired of the teacher. That monotone voice is enough to drive you crazy."

I nodded. I knew what she meant. I'd learned most of my

school stuff through DVD-gigarom too. When I was little, I'd actually talked in a monotone for a while because I thought the voices on the computer were from real people.

"So you began to daydream," I said. "About nothing? Or something?"

For years, I'd envied Earth kids because when they went to school, they could talk to someone. Now, finally, even though it was only a classroom of two, I was in school too. Even if the conversation didn't make much sense.

"This universe," Ashley said, pointing upward through the ceiling of the dome. "Solar system. Mars. Earth. Sun. Why should all of this stuff be here? Why not nothing?"

I peered closely at her. With her short black hair and a serious look on her face, she appeared older than 13. And because her dark brown, almond-shaped eyes could be very unreadable, it was sometimes difficult to figure out if she was joking.

Like now. I waited for her to light up with a big grin, which, when it happened, would change her from mysterious to tomboyish.

"Well?" she said impatiently. She pressed her lips together and squinted at me. "I'm waiting for an answer."

So she wasn't joking.

"Try to picture nothing," Ashley said when all I did was scratch my head.

"Sure," I said. I thought for a second. "Done."

"No," she said. "I disagree. You didn't picture nothing."

I held up my hands in protest. "You can't disagree! You don't even know what I was thinking!"

"Whatever you were thinking was wrong," Ashley said. "You *can't* picture nothing."

"But—"

"You can picture an empty jar. Or maybe a big room with nothing in it. Or even all the space between the stars. But whenever you picture nothing, don't you picture something that's holding all that nothing?"

"Well, maybe I—"

"So why should there be something instead of nothing? You know, all the stuff that makes the stars and the planets. Why can't there be nothing? And where did the something come from? Did it exist forever? But how can something exist forever? If first there was nothing, how did it suddenly become something? I mean, you don't make rocks the size of a planet from empty air. Then think about all the stars and planets in the entire universe. Those came from nothing? Ha! And—"

"Ashley!" I said. "You're making me dizzy."

Finally she grinned. "I'm making myself dizzy."

"At least we agree on *something*."

She nodded, and her tiny silver cross earrings flashed. She reached up to touch them. "I think it's cool to spend time wondering about God and why we're put into this universe."

I returned her nod. It was cool. There are so many mysteries that science is far from figuring out, yet God knows about them. A person could spend a lifetime thinking about God and everything he's done and never get bored.

Ashley closed her handheld computer. "I'm done for the day. How about you?"

I thought of what Rawling had asked me to do. How he'd made me promise not to tell anyone except my parents.

"Me too," I said. "At least with my schoolwork. We've done enough this week that we're ahead, right?"

Ashley nodded again. "Right. Let's go see how Flip and Flop are doing."

Flip and Flop are the little koala-like animals that she and I had rescued from a genetics experiment gone wrong. And just in the nick of time too. It hadn't taken long for the techies at the dome to adopt the friendly creatures as mascots.

"Wish I could," I said, "but I need to ask my parents something."

Ashley shrugged. "See you tonight, then? At the telescope?"

"Sure," I said.

I just hoped—after everything else Rawling had told me—that tonight wouldn't be my last time to see Ashley . . . or anyone else, for that matter.

CHAPTER 5

An hour later, I sat at the computer in my room in the mini-dome I shared with my parents. Aside from my desk, there was a bed. Not much else. Under the dome, everybody wore the standard uniform—a navy blue jumpsuit—so I didn't need a big closet. And because I was always in a wheelchair, I didn't need a chair.

My computer was what made the room alive for me. Through it I learned about Earth, played games, and listened to music, even if most of the songs were 10 years old because the adults picked the playlists. And when the solar system was clear of the electromagnetic particles from solar flares, I could even pick up some Internet transmissions. Although my body was in the prison of a wheelchair, my mind could go almost anywhere.

Tonight, though, I wasn't going to listen to music or read DVD-gigarom books. It had been a week or two since I'd written anything in my journal.

I flicked on the power, and my computer booted up faster than I could count to five. I clicked the right spots, and my writing program opened up.

I began to keyboard my thoughts into my computer journal.

A short while ago, it looked like the entire Mars colony wasn't going to survive because the dome's oxygen level was dropping. At the time, I agreed to write a journal so people on Earth would know about those last days from the viewpoint of a kid instead of a scientist.

We all survived, of course, and I decided to keep a journal about things that happen under the dome. Sometimes I'm too tired to get on my computer to write like this. Other times there doesn't seem to be much to write about, so I spend time up at the telescope.

But with what I've just learned from Rawling, it looks like I'd better not be lazy with my journal. Sometimes I pretend I'm writing a letter to myself, so that when I'm an old man, I can read these letters and remember what it was like to be the first person born on Mars. After all, everybody was surprised when my mother and father fell in love with each other on their eight-month journey to Mars 15 years ago. Once on the planet, they exchanged vows over a radio phone with a preacher on Earth. Then, an Earth year later, the director of the Mars Project, Blaine Steven, was even more shocked when my mom announced she was going to have a baby. It made things really complicated since ships arrive here only every three years, and cargo space is very, very expensive. There was no room for baby items—or a motorized wheelchair.

But you don't have to feel sorry for me. Because of the operation on my spine that went wrong, I'm able to explore Mars and the universe in a way no human in history has ever been able to do—by controlling a robot body. The way it works is . . .

I stopped my keyboarding and let my mind wander to all I was able to do as I controlled the robot body. As I thought about the robot body I named Bruce, I reached down to the small pouch hanging from the armrest of my wheelchair. Pulling out three red balls, I began to juggle, keeping all three in the air. Juggling didn't take much concentration for me. Especially since the gravity was lower on Mars than on Earth.

I kept the red balls in the air for another five minutes, remembering the first time I had sent the robot body outside the dome. Because Bruce delivered sights and sounds and sensations to my mind, it was almost like being outside in my very own body. Although the computer effects were very complicated, the theory was simple.

I stopped juggling the red balls and began to describe it for my journal.

In virtual reality, you put on a surround-sight helmet that gives you a 3-D view of a scene on a computer program. The helmet is wired, so when you turn your head, it directs the computer program to shift the scene as if you were there in real life. Sounds generated by the program reach your ears, making the scene seem even more real. Because you're wearing a wired jacket and gloves, the arms and hands you see in your surround-sight picture move wherever you move your own arms and hands.

But here's what you might not have thought about when it comes to virtual reality: when you take off the surround-sight helmet and the jacket and gloves that are wired to a computer, you're actually still in a virtual-reality suit. Your body.

Rawling was the one who explained it best to me. You see, your brain doesn't see anything. It doesn't hear anything. It doesn't smell anything. It doesn't taste anything. It doesn't feel anything. Instead, it takes all the information that's delivered to it by your nerve endings from your eyes, ears, nose, tongue, or skin and translates that information.

In other words, the body is like an amazing 24-hour-a-day virtual-reality suit that can power itself by eating food and heal itself when parts get cut or broken. It moves on two legs, has two arms to pick things up, and is equipped to give information through all five senses. Except instead of taking you through virtual reality, a made-up world, your body takes you through the real world.

What if your brain could be wired directly into a robot? Then wouldn't you be able to see, hear, and do everything the robot could?

Well, that's me. The first human to be able to control a robot as if it were an extension of the brain. It began with that operation when I was little and . . .

I heard voices outside my room.

My parents.

I quickly saved all I'd written into my journal and rolled out to the common area of our minidome to greet them. I knew

I had some work ahead of me to convince them I should be able to leave the dome with Rawling. And this time, not through a robot that I controlled.

But as myself.

I was excited—and scared.

CHAPTER 6

"A four-day trip away from the dome? That hasn't been done in the last 10 years. And you're saying Rawling wants to travel 200 miles?" My mother looked across at my father with concern on her face.

The three of us sat in the center of our minidome—Mom and Dad in chairs and me, of course, in my wheelchair.

Like every other minidome, ours had two office-bedrooms with a common living space in the middle. Because we only heated nutri tubes, we didn't need a kitchen—only a microwave, which hung on the far wall. Another door at the back of the living space led to a small bathroom. It wasn't much. From what I've read about Earth homes, our minidome had less space in it than two average bedrooms.

"Rawling says we'll take a platform buggy," I answered.

"He'll double up on all the food and oxygen and water just in case anything goes wrong."

Naturally, Mom picked up on the one word a kid should never use when trying to convince his parents of anything.

"Wrong?" she repeated with a quick turn of her head. "What does Rawling think might go wrong?"

As a plant biologist, it was Mom's job to genetically alter Earth plants so they could grow on Mars. Normally she was very businesslike. In fact, until a month ago, when Dad finally returned from a three-year trip to Earth and back, she'd always been satisfied with a hairstyle that didn't take much fussing and gave her as much time as possible for her science. But now she was letting her hair grow longer and making sure it was done nicely. And that wasn't all. I'd noticed more changes in her. With Dad here to complete our family, she was still every bit a no-nonsense scientist, but she seemed more relaxed and happy.

Except when her son had just asked permission to leave the safety of the dome for the dangers of the surface of Mars.

Dad coughed. "Assume the worst and hope for the best. That's a great way to plan for travel. I'm sure Rawling is just taking precautions."

"Yes," I said, glad to have someone on my side. Because Dad had been gone so long, he and I had just learned to be friends again.

"So the bigger question," Dad continued, "is why?"

For me, looking at Dad was almost like looking in a mirror. If I hadn't been in a wheelchair, people would notice I was growing to be as tall as he was. And we both had dark blond hair.

Because I hadn't said anything, Dad repeated his question. "Why does Rawling want to take you on a field trip a couple hundred miles away?"

I cleared my throat. "It's so far from the dome, I wouldn't be able to stay connected to the robot if we tried doing it from here. Rawling needs to load the computer and transmitter on the platform buggy and keep it close enough to the robot so the signal stays strong."

Dad smiled. "Nice try."

"Huh?" I said innocently. He knew me pretty well for someone who had been away from Mars for so long.

"All you did was answer the obvious. What we really want to know is why Rawling wants the robot out there so far from the dome. What does he want it to explore?"

"Oh," I said. "That."

Dad kept smiling. "And . . ."

Rawling had given me permission to tell my parents. But only them. I'd been saving this information for the last. "Rawling asked me to ask you to keep this to yourselves."

Mom and Dad nodded, so I continued. "He thinks that there may be evidence of an alien civilization."

Their reaction was the same that mine had been. Stunned at the thought.

"That's big," Dad said. "Real big."

Mom laughed. "The most staggering discovery in the history of humankind and all you can say is big?"

"What would you say?" he asked, grinning back.

She thought for a moment, opened her mouth to say something, changed her mind, and shut it again. Finally she spoke. "It's big. Real big."

"Exactly," Dad said to her, then turned to me. "It's so big that the only way you can go is if I go too."

CHAPTER 7

That night, as I'd promised Ashley, I went to the dome's telescope. I went early because I loved to spend time alone looking at the Martian night sky.

Earth has an atmosphere that makes the light of the
stars twinkle as it moves through air, but from Mars it's
almost as clear as looking from a spaceship. The lights of the
galaxies are like clusters of diamonds, and the powerful dome
telescope made the view even more incredible, with millions
of tiny bright lights stabbing through the dark of the solar
system.

Whenever I sat at the telescope, I reminded myself
that I was looking backward through time. Light travels at
186,000 miles per second. So if you were riding in a spaceship
that moved at the speed of light, in one minute you'd cover

over 11 million miles. In one hour you'd be 670 million miles from your starting point. In one day you'd be over 16 billion miles away. The scary thing about the size of the universe is that the closest star to Earth is more than four light-years away, which means you'd have to travel at 186,000 miles per second for nearly 1,500 days to get there. (And some stars are millions of light-years away!)

Why is looking through the telescope like looking backward in time?

If you focus on a star a thousand light-years away, the light that hits your eyes left the star a thousand years ago. It might be in the middle of an explosion as you look at it, but you have no way of knowing for another thousand years until the light of that explosion travels billions and billions and billions of miles to reach you.

In short, the farther you look out into the universe, the farther back in time you can see. To me, that's one of the cool things about astronomy.

I rolled into place at the eyepiece of the telescope, where the dome astronomer usually sat. I punched my password into the computer control pad.

It prompted me for a location. The telescope computer was programmed with 100,000 different locations in the universe, as seen from Mars.

Tonight I wanted to look no farther than the backyard of Mars. So I entered *Amors asteroids* into the computer.

The electric telescope motors hummed as the machine automatically swung into place.

Before I was able to lean into the eyepiece, Ashley stepped onto the deck. "Hey," she said. I heard sadness in her voice. I wondered if it had anything to do with her mom and dad. She hadn't talked about it much, but I knew her parents were divorced. "Whatcha looking for?"

"Asteroids," I said. "More specifically, the Amors belt."

Asteroids ranged from the size of a refrigerator to a football stadium to the 15 biggest asteroids, which were each about 150 miles across.

"The Amors belt," she said. "Asteroids in orbit between Mars and Earth."

I grinned. "And the Atens asteroids?"

Ashley paused, beginning to smile because she had a chance to show off her knowledge. "Between Earth and Venus."

"Apollos belt?"

"Much, much more serious. Those are the ones that cross the Earth's orbit."

"Bravo!" I clapped for her.

She bowed as if I were an audience of thousands instead of me, just a kid in a wheelchair beneath the Martian night. "Any reason you picked asteroids? Usually you get us to look at more exciting things like star explosions. Asteroids are just lumpy rocks that drift like garbage."

"Just thinking about the one that might have hit Mars yesterday. Dad and Rawling figure it was only the size of a spaceship."

I stopped, wondering. Could it actually have been a spaceship? One out of control? Made by an alien civilization? What were we going to find when we finally arrived at the crater that the satellite had photographed?

Dumb, I told myself. *Dumb. Dumb. Dumb.* As if an alien spaceship had crashed into Mars.

"Doesn't take much, does it?" Ashley said, breaking into my thoughts. "I mean, I was reading up on asteroids today too, and—"

"Ha!" I interrupted. "That's how you knew about the Amors, Atens, and Apollos belts."

She ignored my comment. "And there's a crater in Arizona nearly a mile across, made by an asteroid fragment only half the size of a football field. If one of the bigger asteroids ever hit Mars, it would break the planet in two!"

"Nice thought," I said.

Ashley shrugged. "At least it would take my mind off the news I just got from Earth." The sadness was back in her voice.

"Is anything the matter?"

"Well—"

Footsteps stopped her from saying anything else.

It was Rawling. "Hi, guys," he said to us. "Sorry to barge

in, but I need to talk to Tyce. It's about our trip. There's no problem if your dad joins us, and we've decided to leave in an hour."

"At night?"

"At night." He didn't give a reason. I thought this was strange. Very strange. Why leave at night?

"So if you could go back down and get ready . . . ," he said.

"Um, sure," I said.

Rawling saluted me and spun around, leaving me and Ashley alone again.

"You were saying?" I said to her.

"Nothing," she said. "Where are you going?"

"On a field trip."

"At night? Nobody's gone out in the field since I got here, and nobody's left the dome at night. What's so important?"

"It's just a field trip."

I could see in her eyes that she was hurt I wouldn't tell her. But I couldn't. Worse, I couldn't even tell her why I couldn't tell her.

"Will you be gone long?" Ashley asked.

"I don't know," I said.

"Oh." She seemed to grow small and quiet. After a few seconds, she reached up and took off one of her silver cross earrings. She handed it to me. "Keep this," she said.

My face must have looked blank.

"You're my only friend under the dome, except for the koalas, and they can't talk. Maybe the cross will also remind you to e-mail me once in a while. I mean, you will have some computers on board, right?"

I smiled again. "Right. But there's nothing to worry about." I paused, thinking about our upcoming search. "Really. Nothing."

Almost as if I were trying to convince myself instead of Ashley.

CHAPTER 8

An hour later, we were ready.

Rawling and Dad had loaded all the supplies into a platform buggy, a clear minidome perched on a deck that rode on huge rubber tires. Storage compartments and the motor were underneath. The motor didn't burn gasoline because Mars has no oxygen in the atmosphere to allow any fuel to burn. Instead, it ran on electricity made from solar panels that hung off the rear of the platform. The minidome looked much like the igloos I've seen in Earth photos. A small tunnel stuck out from the minidome onto an open portion of the deck. Then a ladder descended to the ground from there.

From my wheelchair on the ground I had to lean way back to see the platform. Rawling stayed up there as Dad climbed down. Mom was beside me, her hand on my shoulder, as we waited for Dad to get to us.

He kissed Mom's forehead. "I'll miss you. I'm glad I'm leaving for only a few days, not . . ."

He didn't finish his sentence. In a few more weeks, when the planetary orbits were lined up so the journey from Mars to Earth would be at its shortest, Dad would be on a space-ship again, beginning another three-year journey.

"I'll miss you too." She hugged him. "I'll be praying for you guys."

They kissed again. I coughed and looked the other way.

Mom hugged me and whispered good-bye when they were finished. "Take care of your dad," she said, speaking more loudly for his benefit.

"Sure," I said. But if I had known what was ahead over the next few days, I might not have sounded so cheerful.

The dome was the quietest it had been all day. Dad and Rawling helped me up the ladder onto the platform deck. Rawling went down again and hauled my wheelchair into the buggy. Bruce, the robot body, was already packed underneath.

This late at night, most of the scientists and techies were relaxing in their own minidomes. Because of the quiet, the grinding of the motors that controlled the dome exit seemed louder than usual. The techie who was letting us out waved up to us where we sat high above the ground.

"Ready, gentlemen?" Rawling asked as he waved back at the techie.

"Ready," I said.

Dad's answer was to move levers, rolling the platform buggy into the main dome's igloo tunnel. We left the dome through the inner door and stopped in the short tunnel, which was about twice the length of a platform buggy. Ahead of us, the outer door was still sealed.

The techie closed the inner door behind us, sealing the dome completely. Only then did the techie allow the outer door to open. As the warm, moist, oxygen-filled air followed us out of the dome into the tunnel, it made contact with the Martian atmosphere. Turning instantly into white vapor, it disappeared into the night.

Dad moved the platform buggy forward, and the outer door shut behind us.

We were on our way to search for alien artifacts.

CHAPTER 9

I wasn't worried about getting lost. The platform buggy, which was running off the stored electricity from the dome's solar panels, held a computer with a GPS. The GPS tracked our position by satellite and gave us our coordinates on the surface of the planet at all times. Not only that, but as a space pilot, Dad had managed to get to Mars after crossing 50 million miles of space from Earth—like hitting the head of a pin with a bullet from a thousand miles away. So I figured between him and Rawling, a brilliant scientist, we'd get to the crater, no problem.

"I'm guessing it will take us 14 hours," Rawling said, addressing me. He stood beside Dad at the steering wheel. I sat in my wheelchair to the side, watching through the clear, hard plastic of the platform buggy's dome. "It's about 200 miles.

This buggy can do 25 miles an hour, but we'll want to go slower since it's night. Your dad and I will take turns driving."

I nodded at his time estimate. Since gravity on Mars is much different than gravity on Earth, a year on Mars is much longer than on Earth: Mars takes 687 days to circle the sun. But the length of days is similar. Just like Earth, Mars spins, and it takes 24 hours and 37 minutes to complete each rotation.

"I'm hoping," Rawling continued, "that you'll sleep as much as possible. We need you rested, with a sharp concentration level."

"Sure," I said. Rawling had brought on board the narrow bed from the computer lab. There were also two small roll-out cots for him and Dad. And three space suits with oxygen tanks—one for me in case of emergency and one for each of them so they could walk around when we got to the site.

I watched the passing landscape in the headlight beams for a few more minutes. While Mars has mountains and extinct volcanoes, there are plenty of valleys, so I was seeing landscape almost like a desert on Earth, except here there were no plants of any kind. Just sand and rocks.

The monstrous tires of the platform buggy rumbled as they pressed against the ground. Because of a good suspension system, the platform deck stayed level most of the time, but there were occasional bumps. I was surprised at how soothing the noise and bumps felt. Maybe it was like being rocked to sleep in a cradle—something I'd only read about.

But I wasn't ready to sleep. Not yet.

I asked Rawling the question I'd been saving. "Why did we have to leave tonight in such a big rush?"

"Politics," he answered. "Plain and simple."

Dad kept his eye on the white circles of light cast by the headlight beams.

Rawling gave his attention to me. "Think of what it would mean on Earth if we discovered evidence of an alien civilization. If those black boxes came from beings who once lived on Mars or from beings from another solar system who left them on Mars, this would be the greatest discovery in the history of humankind."

"With our names all over it, right?" I grinned. "We'd be known forever!"

Dad took his eyes off the headlight beams briefly and snorted. "My son, the space explorer." He smiled, shook his head with affection, and kept driving.

"For starters," Rawling explained to me, "if what we find belonged to an ancient Martian civilization, we might be able to learn a tremendous amount about how to recolonize the planet. Did they live underground? Where did they get power? How did they make food? All those answers will be extremely valuable."

"And if these black boxes aren't from a Martian civilization . . ."

"Since no planets other than Mars and Earth are

potentially inhabitable, it means the boxes had to come from outside the solar system. Which would be far more incredible."

"An alien is an alien," I pointed out, "no matter where it's from."

"Not quite," Rawling said. "Aliens from outside this solar system could only get here with some type of transportation that overcomes the tremendous distances. Think about it. With the best technology we have, it still takes three years to catch an orbit to take us from Mars to Earth and back. Imagine being able to travel to the stars."

"Close to light-speed travel!" Dad said. Now, as a space pilot, he was very interested.

"That's a big stretch to conclude from the presence of unexplained black boxes," Rawling cautioned. "But a possible stretch."

"Well," I said, "what does this have to do with politics and the reason we left in such a hurry?"

"If we find evidence of an alien civilization, scientists will be extremely curious to learn from it. And the government will also want to know if it needs to defend Earth against future alien invasions. Given these two factors, how much money do you think the United Nations' Science Agency would be prepared to spend on the Mars Project?"

Even I understood that kind of politics. "Tons and tons and tons," I answered.

Rawling nodded. "Right now, it's costing Earth about $200 billion a year to support the dome. You can bet that money would be doubled or tripled. Or more."

Rawling paused as the platform buggy hit a big bump, then waited for the platform to level itself and stop shaking. "Here's why we couldn't wait until tomorrow to leave. Travel to the crater and back will take up to two days altogether. I'd like at least two days to explore and learn what we can. That gives us four days. Even with that, we'll barely make the deadline."

"Deadline for what?"

"In four days," Rawling told me, "the United Nations is voting on budget issues. Specifically, the amount of money they are going to commit to the Mars Project. We need to find out about this by then or else."

I asked the obvious. "Or else what?"

"It's not public knowledge," Rawling said, "but after all these years and with progress so slow, there are some people on Earth who wonder if the government should be spending $200 billion a year on the dome. When we first left for Mars 15 years ago, we knew that the issue of funding would come up at the end of the 15th year. Now that time is here. As director, I've found out there's a good chance they're going to cut the budget in half at that meeting. Or more. Which will mean the end of the dome as we know it."

He let out a deep breath. "In other words, finding evidence of aliens will ensure that all of us stay on Mars."

CHAPTER 10

Rawling wanted me to get as much sleep as possible. He had already dimmed the interior lights. Now he shut them off completely so only the instrument panels glowed.

I lay on my narrow bed, staring through the clear, hard plastic of the platform dome.

The stars were crisp diamond points against the black velvet of the Martian night. And although Mars does have a moon—in fact, two—neither moon gives much light. They are like giant potatoes—huge lumps of rock, each less than 20 miles across.

As I stared upward, waiting to get tired enough to sleep, I was able to see a solar system sight so beautiful that I felt sorry for people on Earth, because they'll never be able to see it. Not unless they actually leave Earth.

What I saw was a round white-and-blue ball hanging against the eternal darkness. Earth itself. With a telescope from Mars, you can see the swirls of cloud cover and watch hurricanes develop. From the platform buggy, however, I had to rely on my memory of telescope sighting.

The atmosphere that surrounds Earth is minuscule compared to the size of the planet. Yet this thin fabric of nitrogen and oxygen makes life possible. Without atmosphere, there's no water, no conservation of heat.

The angle of the tilt of Earth is perfectly suited to give seasons. The size is perfect too. Bigger planets like Venus have too many volcanoes and erupt so much carbon dioxide that the greenhouse effect heats them to 850 degrees Fahrenheit. Smaller planets like Mercury can't hold their atmosphere.

And Earth's moon? Planets without a large moon flip-flop on the axis of rotation, literally throwing the planet back and forth, making it impossible for life to survive climate changes.

If Earth were only 1 percent closer to the sun (think of taking only 1 penny off a stack of 100 pennies), it would get too hot. Only 5 percent farther away, and it would freeze, like Mars. If the Earth didn't have a nearly perfect circular orbit—always 93 million miles away—it would get too close to and too far from the sun.

In other words, life on Earth only exists because the

planet is the right size, always at the right distance from the right-size sun, with the right-size moon circling it at the right distance.

All of this has convinced me that Earth was created for a reason. And that someone—a powerful Someone, God—made it that way so life could exist. After years of finding it hard to believe in him, I'd been thinking a lot about him over the past month. It had all started with the oxygen crisis and wondering what would happen to me if I died.

I started getting drowsier as these thoughts went through my mind.

Then Ashley's question popped back into my thoughts. *"Why is there something instead of nothing?"*

And what was here instead of the universe before the nothing became something? How can time start? Did it start when the universe started? Or is time forever?

I closed my eyes and let all these questions run through my mind again and again and again.

It must have looked like I was asleep because Rawling and my dad started talking softly.

"It's a big responsibility," Rawling said. "I'm sorry I have to throw it on Tyce's shoulders."

That worried me. What exactly was going to be so difficult?

"It has to be done," Dad answered just as softly. "But if anyone can do it, it's Tyce. Words can't tell you how proud I am to have him as a son."

A month ago, he hardly felt like a father to me. Now it was different. Hearing him say that made me happy.

I fell asleep with a smile on my face.

And I woke up to a loud screeching noise.

CHAPTER 11

The screeching sound was followed by a big jolt of the platform buggy.

In bed, I struggled to sit up. I leaned on my elbows and blinked myself completely awake. The first rays of sun had reached across the horizon, showing the jagged edges of ancient rust-red volcanoes on all sides of us.

"Tyce," Dad said from behind the controls, "you can relax. We're fine."

Rawling was at the side of the platform, peering downward through the clear protective plastic. "I'm not sure about one of our tires though."

The platform deck had begun to tilt in Rawling's direction.

"Some of this lava is sharp as a razor," Rawling continued. "I think it cut one of the rear tires."

Dad leaned back in his chair and rubbed his face. It looked like he'd been at the controls the entire time I'd slept.

"We've got a compressor underneath," Rawling said. "All we need to do is plug the leak with a repair kit, and we'll be on our way."

I remembered the tires were filled with carbon dioxide so we could pump into them straight from the atmosphere.

Dad stood and stretched. "Flip a coin to see who goes out there?"

"Nope," Rawling said. He pointed at me. "Here's where you get to see how good your son is."

"Run through the checklist," Rawling told me as he tightened straps across my legs to hold me to the bed. If I moved, the connection between the antenna plug in my spine and the computer receiver on the other side of the platform deck could be broken.

"First," I said, "no robot contact with any electrical sources. Ever." Because my spinal nerves were attached to the antenna plug, any electrical current going into or through the robot could seriously damage the neurons of my brain. It had happened once—a slight shock—and I'd been out for 6 minutes and 10 seconds.

"Check." We did this every time. Rawling insisted on it. He said on Earth, airline pilots did the same thing before every flight because safety was so important.

Rawling pulled the straps down across my stomach and chest as I continued. "Second, I disengage instantly at the first warning of any damage to the robot's computer drive." My brain circuits worked so closely with the computer circuits during the linkup that harm to the computer could spill over and harm my brain.

"Check." Rawling strapped my head into position.

"How does he disengage?" Dad asked. This was the first time he'd actually seen me at work, though he had unstrapped me once when Rawling was called away. Dad knew the theory behind it, but whenever I'd gone on practice runs, he'd been unable to get away from his own work.

"I shout *Stop!* in my mind," I said. "Sounds strange, but that's all it takes. My brain controls the virtual-reality no differently than it controls my hand muscles or arm muscles."

There's a short, dark rod, hardly thicker than a needle, wedged directly into my spinal column at the bottom of my neck, just above the top of my shoulder blades. From that rod, thousands of tiny biological implants—they look like hairs—stick out of the end of the needle into the middle of my spinal column. Each of the fibers, which have grown into my nerves, has a core that transmits tiny impulses of electricity, allowing my brain to control a robot's computer.

This was part of the long-term plan to develop Mars: to use robots to explore the planet. Humans need oxygen, water, and heat to survive on the surface. Robots don't. But robots can't think like humans. From all my years of training with a computer simulation program, my mind knows the muscle moves it takes to handle the virtual-reality controls. Handling the robot is no different, except instead of actually moving my muscles, I imagine I'm moving the muscles. My brain then sends the proper nerve impulses to the robot, and it moves the way I make the robot move in the virtual-reality computer program.

I admit, it is cool. Almost worth being in a wheelchair. After all, the experimental operation is what caused my legs to be useless.

"Any last questions?" Rawling asked me. "We'll communicate by radio, and I'll direct you on the technical aspects of fixing the tire."

"No questions," I said.

Rawling placed a blindfold over my eyes.

In the darkness that now covered me, I spoke to my dad. "Don't worry. I like this. A lot."

Bruce, the robot, was a freedom that made up for having legs that don't work. No one else could wander the planet like I could.

"Headset?" Rawling asked.

"Headset," I confirmed.

He placed a soundproof headset on my ears. The fewer distractions to reach my brain in my real body, the better.

It was dark and silent while I waited. I knew Rawling

needed to make some computer entries. The antenna plug in my back transmitted and received signals on an invisible X-ray frequency to the computer, which in turn relayed signals to and from the robot body. In my mind, there was no difference between handling the robot and handling a virtual-reality program like any kid on Earth. Except for the fact that the X-ray frequency for the robot had a lot longer range. Like a remote control that could penetrate walls and rock and anything that might get between the computer here and the robot body.

Blindfolded and in the silence of the headset, I waited for a sensation that had become familiar and beautiful for me. The sensation of entering the robot computer.

My wait wasn't long.

In the darkness and silence, I began to fall off a high, invisible cliff into a deep, invisible hole.

I kept falling and falling and falling. . . .

CHAPTER 12

Directly beneath the platform deck, the robot's four video lenses opened. Light patterns were translated digitally and became electrical impulses that followed the electronic circuitry into the computer drive of the robot. From there, they were translated into X-ray waves that traveled to the receiver above. The receiver then beamed to the wires of my jumpsuit, which were connected to the antenna plug in my spine. The electrical impulses moved instantly up the nerves of my spinal column into my brain, which translated the light patterns into images—the same thing it did when light entered my real eyes and hit the optical nerves that reached into my brain.

Although the lenses didn't blink, in my mind, it felt like I blinked into focus.

The monstrous tires of the platform buggy filled most of my view. I saw the lightweight titanium and graphite support beams of the underside of the platform.

The sound of wind and sand drifting across sand reached the robot's intake microphones and translated into sound in my mind.

I thought about moving the robot arms. And instantly it happened. I brought both titanium hands up in front of a video lens and flexed the robot's fingers, wiggling them to make sure everything worked properly.

Everything did.

The robot body hung in a suspended cage. I pushed the button that lowered it. When the cage gently rested on the ground, I pushed another button that opened the door and rolled the robot onto the surface of Mars. The platform buggy was like a giant wagon above me, so I moved away, out from under the wheels and storage compartments, far enough to be able to see the entire minidome.

I waved upward at Rawling and Dad, who were looking for me.

It was weird, seeing them wave back down while only a few feet from them my actual body was motionless on the bed.

I knew how the robot body looked to them. The lower body is much like my wheelchair. Except that instead of a pair of legs, there is an axle that connects two wheels. The robot's upper body is merely a short, thick, hollow pole that sticks through the axle, with a heavy weight to counter-balance the arms and head. Within this weight is the battery that powers the robot, with wires running up inside the hollow pole.

The upper end of the pole has a crosspiece to which arms are attached. They are able to swing freely without hitting the wheels. Like the rest of the robot, they are made of titanium and jointed like human arms, with one difference. All the joints swivel. The hands, too, are like human hands, but with only three fingers and a thumb instead of four fingers and a thumb.

Four video lenses at the top of the pole serve as eyes. One faces forward, one backward, and one to each side.

Three tiny microphones, attached to the underside of the video lenses, play the role of ears, taking sound in. A speaker on the underside of the video lens that faces forward produces sound and allows me to make my voice heard.

The computer drive of the robot is well protected within the hollow titanium pole that serves as the robot's upper body. Since it is mounted on shock absorbers, the robot can fall 10 feet without shaking the computer drive. This computer drive has a short antenna plug-in at the back of the pole to give and take X-ray signals.

The robot is amazing. It has heat sensors that detect infrared, so I can see in total darkness. The video lenses' telescoping is powerful enough that I can recognize a person's face from five miles away. But I can zoom in close on something nearby and look at it as if using a microscope.

I can amplify hearing and pick up sounds at higher and lower levels than human hearing. The fibers wired into the titanium let me feel dust falling, if I want to concentrate on that minute of a level. The fibers also let me speak easily, just as if I were using a microphone.

The robot can't smell or taste, however. But one of the fingers is wired to perform material testing. All I need are a few specks of the material, and this finger will heat up, burn the material, and analyze the contents.

The robot is strong too. The titanium hands can grip a steel bar and bend it.

Did I mention it's fast? Its wheels will move three times faster than any human can sprint. But this morning, I had nowhere to go. My job was very simple. Fix a tire.

Rawling had placed a communications radio just outside the dome of the platform buggy. I saw him lift his radio to his mouth. Instantly, my radio speaker rumbled with his voice.

"Tyce, check the tire to see if the leak is obvious."

I rolled over to the collapsed tire and scanned it with my video lens. "Nothing unusual," I reported in my robot voice. "Can you roll the platform buggy ahead?"

Moments later, it rolled forward in a lopsided way.

Immediately, as the part of the tire that had been resting on the ground came into view, I saw the reason for the screeching sound.

As Rawling had guessed, a long, narrow piece of lava rock stuck from the tire. In fact, it stuck out so far that it scraped the underside of the platform deck each time the tire rolled over.

"Got it!" I said.

I explained what I saw.

With lots of instruction from Rawling, the strong robot hands and arms, and all the right equipment, I was able to seal the leak and refill the tire with compressed carbon dioxide.

It was a simple, routine piece of work.

The only unusual thing about it was a small gray box. I noticed it was attached to the axle of the wheel. I wondered if it was part of the GPS, because it had some wires sticking out, like communications antennae.

I loaded the robot body and raised the cage off the ground so the robot would hang and swing in safety. Then I gave the stop command to disengage from the computer program that controlled the robot.

From the bed inside the platform buggy's minidome, I calmly told Rawling I was ready to be unstrapped.

Seconds later, someone took off my headset and my blindfold.

It wasn't Rawling. It was Dad.

Rawling was at the base radio. Talking.

And when I heard what he said, I forgot all about that small gray plastic box beneath the platform deck.

CHAPTER 13

"Blaine Steven has taken control of the dome?" I heard Rawling say, disbelief in his voice. "He has no authority to do that!"

Blaine Steven? Ex-director? But he was under guard until the next spaceship left Mars to take him to Earth.

"Sir," the communications techie said, "half an hour ago, we received a transmission from Earth. It has the proper electronic identification code that identifies it as a Science Agency message. It granted Blaine Steven full directorship in your absence. It—"

Sudden silence.

"Platform one to main base," Rawling said, trying to get the communications techie back. "Platform one to main base."

"Dr. McTigre." The sound of the radio communications

was tinny, but I still recognized the new voice. Blaine Steven. He'd lost his position over a month ago because of how he'd mishandled an oxygen level zero situation that nearly killed 180 people under the dome. And now he was back?

"This is Rawling." There was controlled anger in his voice.

"And this is Director Blaine Steven. Our computer shows your position clearly. Please explain to me what you are doing so far from base."

Rawling opened and closed his mouth several times.

"That is an order, Dr. McTigre."

I thought I understood Rawling's confusion. If it was true that the Science Agency had reinstated Blaine Steven as director, Rawling had no choice. The director of the dome was like a five-star general in the military. But could Rawling believe the Science Agency had given Blaine Steven the authority?

"That is an order, Dr. McTigre. If you do not respond, I will consider this mutiny."

Mutiny. The worst possible offense under the dome. With penalties so severe that the person would not only be sent back to Earth but also be placed in prison for life.

Rawling shook his head at us and frowned. Then he sighed and said into the radio microphone, "I would rather not explain over the airwaves. However, if you check the logbook on my computer, you will see the urgency of this situation."

Blaine Steven's voice became less harsh. "You're a good man, McTigre. I know you wouldn't be out there without good reason. I will review the logbook. In the meantime, continue with your mission unless you receive a direct order from me to return. I am in control now and will not permit unauthorized field trips. Understood?"

Rawling's jaw clenched with anger. "Understood."

"And I want reports every six hours. Understood?" Steven demanded.

"Understood."

"Good-bye." Blaine Steven clicked off without even waiting for Rawling to say good-bye.

Rawling hung up the radio microphone. "This doesn't make sense," he said, lifting his eyes first to Dad's, then to mine. "No sense at all."

CHAPTER 14

I stood at the edge of the crater in the robot body. Below were boulders and rocks, darker red than most Martian rocks because they'd been so recently exposed to the surface by the explosion that had caused the crater.

About 12 miles away, a mountain range filled my view, almost bright red with late afternoon sun. The temperature was warm for Mars, about 40 degrees Fahrenheit, and just a little windy.

Behind me, towering above Bruce's titanium shell, was the platform buggy. It threw long shadows across the robot body and into the crater. We'd traveled most of the rest of the day because repairing the tire had delayed our arrival here. Now the sun was only two hours away from setting.

To begin, Rawling had given me a simple assignment.
All he needed was a quick survey. With night coming so
soon, he didn't think we'd be able to get much else done.

A thin metal cable was attached to the frame of
the platform buggy. This cable dangled over the edge of
the crater and all the way to the bottom. Just like in my
earlier practice run of cliff climbing when I was carrying
the crash-test dummy, I held grippers in each hand, ready
to clamp the wire as I let myself down to the bottom of the
crater.

Five large black boxes were centered down there among
the boulders and rocks.

Had an ancient Martian civilization left them behind?
Had aliens from outside the solar system hidden them there?
What was inside those mysterious boxes?

It was my job to find out.

Slowly I climbed down the cable hand by hand. The
wheels of my robot body moved easily, and the entire descent
went without any trouble.

Ten minutes later I was on the floor of the crater. It was
almost like being in a maze. The boulders were large enough
that I couldn't see over the tops of them. In many places,
they were so close together that I couldn't roll between them.
I was forced to backtrack and look for other ways around
them.

It had been easy enough to see the large black boxes

from above. They formed the center of a large ring of the boulders, as if the explosion had left them there and thrown the rocks and boulders outward. So seeing the center of the crater from above had been easy.

Down here, though, with the rough, rust-colored rock of the boulders blocking my view in every direction, it was more difficult.

It took 10 more minutes of wandering around the huge boulders before I finally arrived at the opening of the center of the crater.

I got my first close look at the black boxes. Was it the first time a human had seen them?

As I rolled the robot body toward them, I was confident Dad and Rawling were seeing them too through the video lenses that served as the robot's eyes. They recorded everything on a monitor that Dad and Rawling could watch as I moved around.

They, however, could *only* watch.

I could do much more. Like get so close that the huge black boxes surrounded me like a prison wall. Close up, the black of the sides of the boxes was dull. Not dull like weathered paint but a black that seemed to soak up light.

I tapped the side of the nearest box. I don't know what I was expecting. To hear if it was hollow, maybe.

I did not, however, expect the box to start moving.

Which it did. If the robot body had had a heart, it would

have stopped in shock. Because silently the box seemed to split at the corner nearest me. And slowly, very slowly, the sides of the box began to separate.

CHAPTER 15

I scooted backward, letting my video lens roam up and down as the split in the box grew wider and wider.

Down here the crater was filled with shadows because of the angle of the sun. It was difficult to see inside the black box as it opened.

I was ready for anything.

Would an alien charge out at me, awakened from hundreds or thousands of centuries of hibernation?

Would a preprogrammed robot appear with instructions?

Had I triggered a 3-D hologram to speak to me?

Would there be something so totally beyond human culture that I wouldn't be able to understand what I was seeing?

The sides continued to open. Still I saw nothing but blackness in the interior of the box.

I wasn't worried about my own safety. I was in the robot body. All I had to do was shout *Stop!* in my mind, and I'd instantly disengage from controlling the robot. If anything harmed the robot body, which would be difficult to do anyway, my brain and my own body would still be safe in the platform buggy.

Finally, the box stopped all movement.

I waited.

Nothing happened.

I rolled closer again. Cautiously.

Nothing happened.

Still closer.

The inside of the box seemed to soak up all light. In the shadows of the crater, it was like looking into an infinitely deep cave.

Still closer. I stopped about 20 feet from the open black box.

Then I saw it, floating in the air. In the exact center of the box. It was a round object the size of a human head.

I knew what Rawling would want me to do at this point: zoom in closer with my video lens and record the object for him and Dad to examine on the monitor. I focused closer and opened the video lens as wide as possible to capture as much light as it could.

That's when I saw the object was not a head. It was

more like a gyroscope globe—a wheel or disk that spins rapidly around an axis—and made of thin, curved, shiny tubing. It rotated slowly. But the weirdest part was that it just hung there, in the center of the box, like it was defying gravity.

That's all I could see inside this huge black box.

I had my instructions from Rawling. "Just observe and record," he'd said firmly. "Disengage at the first sign of danger. Let the video lenses do the work. Do not interfere with anything."

I had to know, however. Was that rotating globe hanging from something?

I wondered about waiting until I'd discussed it with Rawling. But what if the black box closed? What if exposure to the Martian atmosphere damaged it?

I decided to get as close as possible. I rolled forward until I was almost at the black box.

The gleaming globe hung there, like a silent eye staring back at me. I saw that it rotated from left to right, then up and down, then right to left, then down and up.

How could it rotate in so many different directions if it was hanging from something like a black wire hidden in the darkness of the box? But if nothing was holding it, how could it hang there against the force of gravity?

I wasn't going to touch the globe. No, I had Rawling's instructions. All I wanted to do was pass the titanium hand of the robot body over the top of the suspended globe. I wanted to see if somehow something was holding it in place.

So I carefully reached into the box.

And my entire world exploded.

CHAPTER 16

I woke to darkness.

Not the darkness of the blindfold that covered my own eyes. But the darkness of the Martian night, with the pinpoints of light—the stars—coming through the clear plastic of the platform buggy's minidome.

"Hello?" I croaked. "Hello?"

I heard the sound of footsteps as Rawling and Dad both rushed toward me.

"Tyce!" Dad said. I heard the worry in his voice.

"Tyce!" Rawling said a millisecond later.

The loudness of both their voices struck like a sledgehammer to the side of my head. "Whisper," I pleaded. "Just whisper."

A tiny light appeared in Rawling's hand. "I want to

check your pupils." He beamed the light in my eye. "Better. Much better."

"It was worse?" I asked as I lay on the bed with Dad and Rawling now beside me.

"Somehow a massive electrical current short-circuited the robot computer drive. For you, it was the equivalent of running your head into a wall."

"Felt like it," I said, groaning.

"How's everything else?" Rawling asked. "Fingers, hands, arms. Start moving."

I sat up carefully. "Oh no!"

"What?" Dad asked. "What is it?"

"My legs! I can't move them!" I stopped, pausing dramatically. "Forgot. I couldn't move them before either."

"Very funny," Dad growled. "Very, very funny."

I thought it was. I mean, if I couldn't joke about being in a wheelchair, then it meant I was feeling too sorry for myself. I'd learned to accept it a long time ago.

Dad helped me into my wheelchair.

Rawling had moved to the platform buggy controls. He turned up the interior lights. "Let's talk," he said, pulling up a chair beside me.

Dad did the same so that we formed a small semicircle.

"We have everything on video until you reached inside," Rawling continued. "Then the short-circuit cut everything out. I thought you'd promised not to touch or interfere with anything you saw."

I nodded. I explained that all I'd wanted to do was see if the thing was floating. I hadn't intended to touch anything at all.

"Maybe there was some kind of protective force field," I said.

"Maybe," Rawling said. "But we won't find out until tomorrow. Your dad's going to go down there in a protective suit and pull the robot body away from the black boxes. Hopefully all he'll need to do is replace a circuit breaker in the computer hard drive and Bruce will be ready again. But we can't have you knocking yourself out. No damage was done this time, but next time . . ." He didn't need to finish his statement.

"What do you think that globe was?" I asked. We were still speaking in low voices. Not only was it easier on my headache, but it seemed to fit. After all, we were 200 miles away from the main dome, sheltered from the Martian night only by a thin layer of plastic that held in the warmth and oxygen we needed to live. We were alone and isolated in the dark, only a stone's throw from a mysterious set of objects that might have been left in the crater by aliens.

"We've reviewed the videos again and again," Dad said. "We're afraid to let ourselves believe what we think it is. Rawling doesn't want to send a satellite feed of the video to the main dome yet, even though Blaine Steven has gone from asking for reports every six hours to calling us every hour. Because if it's what we think it is . . ."

Rawling let out a deep breath. "You see, Tyce, we have no idea how long those black boxes have been buried. No idea how long that globe has been spinning and spinning. For all we know, it's been there for thousands of years, waiting for someone to discover it."

"Have you heard of a perpetual motion machine?" Dad asked me.

"I've heard about people trying to find a way to make one," I said. "It's a machine that never loses energy. It'll stay in motion forever."

"Right," he said. "Inventors on Earth have been trying to come up with one for centuries. Tell me, why is it impossible to make one?"

"Easy," I said. "Friction. No matter how efficient a machine is, it will lose energy as it fights friction. The moving parts inside cause friction. Air outside causes friction. Contact with the ground will cause friction."

"What if the machine has some force that actually allows it to act against gravity?" Dad asked. "Then what?"

"Antigravity. That's as impossible as perpetual motion."

Neither replied.

"No way," I said. "You think this thing has both? Anti-gravity *and* some energy source to allow perpetual motion?"

"How else can you explain it?" Rawling said, scratching his head in thought. "We've run the video in slow motion and reviewed it dozens of times. This *thing* has no apparent source of power and nothing to hold it in place. Yet we can't guess how long it's been spinning against gravity."

"Wow," I said. "It must be alien."

"That fact alone would be staggering beyond belief," Dad said. "But if somehow humankind could understand how to make an antigravity force, it would change our history forever. We could put buildings together that don't need support. Transporting goods would be cheap. People might travel in the air as easily as walking across a street. Add on top of that a way to keep a machine in motion without losing energy and . . ."

Rawling shook his head in awe. "If that's truly what it is, I don't think we can comprehend how much this means to the human race."

CHAPTER 17

"I don't think we can comprehend how much this means to the human race."

As I tried to sleep, Rawling's words echoed again and again in my mind.

Antigravity? Without gravity holding them down, cars and trains would move with no more than the push of a fingertip. Airplanes would be weightless. It would change all types of transportation so fuel would barely be needed. And what if small antigravity devices were made so people could float?

Wow! If scientists could figure out what made that globe revolve, they might be able to apply the principle of perpetual motion to large motors. What would Earth be like without fights over energy?

The whole purpose of the Mars colony was to help the overpopulated world. It was expected to take 100 years or more. In that time, millions of people might die from starvation or war.

And now?

Just maybe, machines with antigravity or perpetual motion motors might solve the problems. Lives would be saved. Earth would be saved.

Thinking about all this, I couldn't sleep. I twisted and turned in my bed.

I saw that Dad was sitting near the side of the platform, staring through the clear plastic at the dark, still Martian landscape.

"Dad?" I whispered.

"Yes, Tyce," he whispered back.

"You can't sleep either?"

He laughed softly. "Just thinking."

"Me too," I said.

Dad stood. He rolled my wheelchair toward me and stopped it near the bed. He sat in it, facing me. "Thinking about what?"

"How what we've discovered might solve so many problems for humans."

Dad was quiet for so long, I wondered if he'd heard me. He sighed. "A lot of people will think that. But they'll be wrong."

"Wrong?" I asked. I propped myself up on my elbows. Above me, the stars were intense against the black sky.

"It's sad and funny," he answered. "For as long as there have been people, we humans have always looked for ways to make the perfect society. And we've always failed. People think the next solution will work, but it never does."

"The perfect society?"

"Everybody happy. No wars, no crime. Enough property and resources shared so people aren't greedy or hateful. For the last four centuries, science has tried to accomplish that. Better medicine. Better computers. Better psychiatry. And on and on and on. But nothing works."

"Antigravity," I protested. "Machines that conserve energy forever. Now people won't need to fight or steal, right?"

"Wrong. You know we've had talks about this. Humans have souls, Tyce. We're empty without God to fill us. We keep looking for other solutions because we don't want to admit the need." Dad laughed again. "So people on Earth are going to hear about this and think we've been saved. By aliens. They're going to be more willing to believe in aliens than in God. But I'll tell you what. They can have all the money, power, and resources in the world, and they'll still feel like they're missing something. Antigravity machines or perpetual motion machines aren't the answer."

I thought that over. "That's why you and Mom aren't afraid, isn't it?"

"It's a matter of perspective. Finding peace with God, looking at life as something beyond satisfying hunger and pleasure."

I ran my fingers over Ashley's silver cross earring, which hung on the chain around my neck.

"Tyce?"

I guess I'd been quiet for a few minutes. "Dad?"

We were still whispering.

"That make sense to you?"

I smiled in the darkness. "Yeah, it does."

CHAPTER 18

"Done?" Rawling said into the handheld communication device.

"Done." It was my dad's voice. He was in the crater, in his space suit, with a handheld too. "Your guess was correct, Rawling. All it took was a fuse."

A few minutes earlier, Dad had reported finding the robot body frozen in place a few paces back from the mysterious black box, which he'd found closed.

"Good," Rawling answered. "Box still closed?"

"Still closed." There was a pause. "It's opening again. All I did was tap it, just like Tyce did yesterday."

"Good again. And the antigravity gyroscope globe?"

"Hang on. The door's still opening. It's . . . it's . . . yes. It's still there."

"I'll send Tyce right down," Rawling said. He nodded in my direction.

I was already on the bed, my legs strapped into place. I'd been awake since dawn, waiting for this chance.

Rawling stepped over to the bed. We went through the regular checklist as he got me ready.

"The other boxes are opening too," Dad said into his handheld.

Now I was on my back, blindfold over my eyes.

"I can't believe this," Dad said. "I just can't believe this! Get Tyce here as fast as you can!"

Rawling slipped the headset over my ears.

Ten seconds later, I began that deep fall into deep black.

Light entered the robot body's video lenses.

I scanned four directions. The boulders were behind me, with one black box open directly in front of them. The gyroscope globe still floated and rotated in its eerie, awesome way. I knew better than to reach inside that black box.

"Dad?" I said through the robot voice speaker. "Dad?"

"Over here, Tyce!" His voice was muffled coming out of his space helmet. "Get ready to record all this!"

Dad was around the corner of the black box open in front of me. In his space suit, he looked like a marshmallow man. He pointed at the inside of the box as I rolled into his sight.

The edges of the box threw dark, crisp shadows on the rocky soil. But I didn't spend much time admiring the blue of the sun or the butterscotch of the sky.

Not with what caught my eye.

Aliens!

Human-size aliens! Frozen in position. Two of them.

They were like giant ants with six arms and a two-sectioned body instead of three. In place of an antlike head, however, each had a smooth, egg-shaped face. Their eyes were black. Two, like a human, but easily five times the size of human eyes, and on the bottom of the face. Black, gaping holes were open wide on their foreheads.

Neither wore clothing or anything that I recognized as clothing. Each was coated with a layer of thick, clear plastic. The material might not have been plastic, but that's the only way I could describe it.

Their arms were tucked against their sides. I wondered if they were alive.

"Hibernation?" I asked Dad. "Or dead and buried like this?"

"I don't know," Dad said. "All the other boxes are identical. Two per box. Except for the one box you opened yesterday. That holds the antigravity gyroscope globe."

I scanned the inside of the box with the robot's video lenses, trusting all this was showing up on Rawling's monitor back on the platform buggy.

I went from box to box, doing the same with each. Dad was right. There were two aliens per box, each about the same size.

I wondered what had happened. Maybe they'd allowed themselves to be sealed, expecting that someday other aliens would come back and revive them.

Or maybe they'd been killed and thrown into the boxes, like prisoners of some intergalactic war.

Or maybe they were old and had died of natural causes, and the clear plastic coating was the alien way of mummifying them.

Or maybe . . .

"Tyce!" Dad shouted in panic.

I reversed the robot and sped as fast as I could in the direction of his voice.

I reached Dad quickly and stared at the inside of the box he pointed at. The alien forms were beginning to melt down, as if an invisible fire had taken hold of them.

Five seconds later, the box itself exploded, knocking me backward and slamming me into a boulder.

As the robot body wobbled back into balance, a second box exploded. Then a third. And a fourth. And a fifth.

After that, the ground began to slide into itself, as if it were water in slow motion, going down a drain.

"Dad!" I yelled. "Dad!"

CHAPTER 19

I wheeled in tight circles until I found Dad.

The blast had thrown him against a boulder. His eyes were closed, and he was slumped and limp. His space helmet was cracked, and blood trickled from the corner of his mouth.

Since everyone at the dome is required to take first aid, I knew one of the first rules was not to move the injured person. But that only applied if the person wasn't in further danger where he was.

In this case, with the ground slipping away, I had to move Dad quickly.

I knew his space helmet was fine for now. If the crack had gone all the way through, I'd be seeing a hiss of vapor as the moist, oxygen-filled air of his space suit leaked away, along with his life.

I didn't know about his back. He could have broken it. Under ideal circumstances, two men would carefully place him on a stretcher and strap him so he was immobile.

These were not ideal circumstances.

Whatever booby trap the aliens had left, it was working quickly. It felt like a hole had opened beneath the circle where the black boxes had been. The hole was sucking sand and small rocks downward.

With the robot's titanium arms, I lifted Dad as gently as I could.

I spun a tight circle, grateful that the robot had strength I'd never hope to get in my own body.

The cable hung over the edge of the crater. Earlier, when Dad had gone into the crater to fix the robot's computer drive, he'd climbed down alone, using the grippers. Now the robot would have to carry him.

I raced to the cable, fighting the moving rivers of sand that tried to pull me down into the hole.

Only then did I realize how much trouble this would be. I couldn't strap Dad to my back. In the practice runs, Rawling and I had assumed that any passengers would strap themselves into place.

Dad was unconscious.

And the sand began to suck at my robot wheels.

In my mind, I shouted *Stop!* to disengage myself from the robot controls.

I woke up in the platform buggy.

"Rawling," I said into the darkness and the silence. I was blindfolded and in the headset, so I had to trust he'd listen. "You've seen what happened on the monitors. I need to get Dad back up. But I can't without your help. Back the platform buggy away from the edge of the crater. Now!"

With time running out for Dad, I was glad Rawling had made me go on so many practice runs. I knew how to slip back into the virtual reality of the robot controls without his coaching.

Into the darkness, I began to fall. . . .

Light entered the robot's video lenses.

Straight ahead were the red rock walls of the crater. The cable dangled in front. And in the robot's arms was my dad's quiet body.

I grabbed the cable with a gripper clamp in the robot's right hand and held Dad firmly in the left arm. I braced myself, hoping Rawling understood what I needed.

Seconds later, sand disappeared from under me.

Because I was hanging on to the cable, I didn't roll backward with the sand.

Soon after that, the cable lurched upward as Rawling eased the platform buggy away from the crater.

I held on, letting him tow the robot body and Dad up the crater wall. The robot wheels rolled smoothly.

I kept a good grip on Dad and rode the cable all the way up the wall until the cable finally towed me over the edge and onto the safe, flat ground.

Instantly I released the cable and raced toward the platform buggy.

When I got there, Rawling was already in a space suit and climbing down to help me with Dad.

CHAPTER 20

"All I've got is a doozy of a headache," Dad said. His grin was weak, and Rawling had wiped the blood off his pale face. "Nothing worse. Really. We probably don't even have to mention this to your mother."

Dad woke up 10 minutes after Rawling and I had helped him out of his space suit within the safety of the platform buggy's minidome. Rawling revived Dad with smelling salts from the first-aid kit.

Several hours passed while Dad recovered. During that time, the three of us watched the digital video scans over and over.

Now Rawling was at the controls of the platform buggy, driving us back in the direction of the main dome.

Dad and I sat facing the monitor. With the remote in his hand, Dad again clicked the digital video scan replay, and images flickered onto the screen. I saw on the monitor everything that the robot body had relayed up to the computer on the platform buggy.

The camera surveyed the first alien bodies up and down. It did the same with the other bodies in the other black boxes. Then the background blurred during the section where I'd raced back to the first bodies, which then began to melt.

Dad clicked the slow-motion button. "It's as if some kind of chemical reaction is taking place. Like the bodies were sealed until we opened the boxes."

"And then," Rawling added as he continued to drive, "the carbon dioxide of Mars's atmosphere must have reacted with a substance on the clear coating, turning it into an acid. . . . Hold on. I have to talk to Steven." Rawling called up the main dome on our field radio.

While Rawling was patched in to Blaine Steven, I kept my eyes on the monitor, only half listening to Rawling's report.

"We'll relay all the video images immediately," Rawling said to Steven. "It appears the artifacts had some sort of self-destruct timer. Everything was destroyed, but we've got it all on video."

On the monitor, the first box exploded outward.

"Can you back up a few frames and go to super slow motion?" I asked Dad.

As Dad clicked back a few frames, Rawling continued to drive and speak into the field radio at the front of the platform.

"Please confirm by calling back when you receive the satellite relay," Rawling told Blaine Steven. "I don't want to imagine the worst, but if anything should happen to us on the way back to the dome, I want to know that copies of the video footage are safe with you. What we saw down there was absolutely incredible. This can't be lost to the rest of humankind."

Again, I was barely listening to Rawling. I was watching hard for the source of the explosion. Because the digital video scan was advancing frame by frame, in the first instant of the explosion I was able to see the first bloom of bright light in the bottom rear of the black box.

"Stop," I told Dad. "Back it up again. Two frames. Then hold."

"Yes," Rawling was saying. "Unfortunately, there's no other evidence but the video feed. Once you have it, you've got all that we've got. But it should be enough to convince the Science Agency committee that something incredible is here. Somehow those aliens had the technology for antigravity and perpetual motion."

I wasn't sure if I saw on the monitor what my mind thought I saw.

"We'll be back as soon as possible," Rawling said. "See you then."

"Stop!" I shouted, suddenly afraid.

Rawling hung up the radio speaker.

"But I've got it stopped," Dad said to me. The frame was frozen on the monitor.

"No," I said. "Stop the platform buggy! Now!"

There, on the monitor, in the back corner of one of the black boxes, was a small, gray, plastic box with antennae.

If I was right, that little gray box on the monitor had triggered the explosion that began in the next frame. And it was just like the one I'd seen on the axle of the platform buggy when I fixed the tire.

How long did we have until it exploded beneath us?

CHAPTER 21

Whoever this is, you are mean and nasty and rotten to pretend you are Tyce Sanders. Respect the memory of his death. Get off his computer and leave it alone. He was a true space hero. And he was my friend. I miss him very much. Please do not send me another e-mail.

I stared at the screen of the mainframe computer on the platform buggy. We were parked about five miles from the dome, behind a range of short mountains. It was the middle of the day, and I'd sent Ashley an e-mail on this computer about 10 minutes earlier.

I grinned at Ashley's return message. I could picture her and her mad frown as she banged at her keyboard. I was glad to read that she liked me.

I hit Reply. All the dome's computers were set up with an Internet system that let scientists and techies send each other e-mails.

The reply box appeared on my computer screen.

Ashley,

It really is me. I know that everyone under the dome thinks we're dead. And my guess is that Blaine Steven announced it, right? But we're alive. It's important you keep this secret. Please e-mail me back and tell me that you will help.

I pressed Send.

Rawling and Dad were snoozing on the platform beds behind me. Taking turns, they had driven all of the previous night and the beginning of this day to get here.

But our mission wasn't finished.

We couldn't let anyone at the dome see the platform buggy. We guessed by now that they all believed it had been blown up in a mysterious accident. Dad was upset thinking how sad Mom must be. He wanted to get back to the dome as soon as possible to let her know we were alive. The thought of how Mom must be feeling tore me up inside too.

But we had to wait. On the long drive back, Dad and Rawling had begun to guess what had happened. If they were right, we'd find out soon. But only with Ashley's help.

The computer chirped.

If you don't stop with these messages, I'll go straight to the director. He'll track the message to see where it came from. I'll make sure you're punished. How could you dare pretend to be Tyce? Don't send me any more messages . . . please.

I knew by now that Mom would be crying. Dad and I wanted to send an e-mail to her, but Rawling asked us to wait just a few hours. He was afraid that if Mom showed happiness or excitement, then Director Steven might wonder what was happening.

And it was Blaine Steven who we needed to get. By himself. Away from the dome.

But how could I convince Ashley to help us? How could I convince her that I was alive and the e-mails truly were coming from me?

I remembered something. I reached into my pocket and held it in my hand.

You gave me one of your silver earrings. Remember?

I hit Send. Snores reached me. What was it about adults that made them snore? And what about those hairs on their shoulders and the backs of their arms? And the nostril hairs? And . . .

Her reply came 30 seconds later.

Tyce? I want so badly to believe it's you. But maybe the real Tyce told someone about the earring before leaving the dome. Maybe you heard about it and are pretending to be him, which would be the meanest thing in the world to do. So if you are Tyce Sanders, tell me what question I asked you on the day you left the dome.

I grinned. How could I forget her question? It was something to think about whenever I could, especially after what Dad and I had talked about.

I began to keyboard a reply.

Why is there something instead of nothing? Why not nothing? And where did the something come from? Did it exist forever? But how can something exist forever? But if first there was nothing, how did the nothing suddenly become something? How can stars and planets just come from empty air?

Once again, I sent the message. I leaned back in my wheelchair and waited.

The snoring behind me grew louder as Dad and Rawling fell deeper and deeper into sleep.

The computer chirped. I scanned her message.

Tyce,

It is you! What happened? I mean, at the dome Director Steven announced that the platform buggy had exploded. He said there was no GPS signal, so you weren't traceable. The satellite photos showed a small crater where the platform buggy had sent its last signal. But if it didn't explode, why have you guys let everyone at the dome think you are dead?

I leaned forward in my wheelchair. Rawling had jotted down on a piece of paper the instructions to give to Ashley. I decided to dash off a quick e-mail to her before I began to keyboard them in.

Don't let anyone know we are alive. Tonight they'll find out anyway, and then I can explain. But first you need to help us. At 8:00 tonight, go to the dome entrance. Let me in without anyone knowing it. In the meantime, I'll be sending another long e-mail with more instructions.

Again, I sent the message.

I thought about our plan. The dome entrance had two

ways of getting in. The first, of course, was through the large doors that allowed platform buggies in and out of the dome. The second was a normal-size door so techies and scientists could just walk out in space suits.

I'll keep it a secret. (So will Flip and Flop! They're sitting right beside me.) And I'll meet you there at 8:00. I think I know a way to get you in secretly. See you then.

Your happy, happy friend,
Ashley

I sighed with satisfaction. Dad and Rawling would be happy to hear it too. If the rest of our plan worked, it would be great. If not . . .

I didn't want to think about it. Actually, it was tough to think about anything. Not with how both of them snored.

I tore a little strip of paper off the note Rawling had written. I wheeled over to where Dad was asleep and snoring like a chainsaw. I tickled the inside of his nostril with the paper.

Asleep, he swatted at it.

I tickled more.

He snorted and grunted and finally hit himself in the nose so hard that it woke him up.

"Hi," I said innocently. "Want to hear about Ashley?"

CHAPTER 22

"What nonsense is this? Calling me here this late at night?"

The angry hiss belonged to Director Blaine Steven. He directed his questions to Ashley, who sat quietly on a bench near the tall, thick plants in the center of the dome, where she and I had met just an hour earlier.

"Thank you for coming," she said sweetly.

It was dim. This late—just before 9:00—the dome lights were turned down. Most scientists and techies were reading or at their personal computers or getting ready to sleep. At the dome, the policy was early to bed and early to rise.

"I wouldn't be here if you hadn't sent that crazy message," Director Steven continued in his low growl. Steven, who was over 60, ran his hands through his thick, wavy gray hair as he talked. "What do you mean Tyce Sanders sent you a message?"

"The aliens are fake," Ashley said bluntly. "When an asteroid hit nearby, causing a quake, someone here triggered a bomb that exposed the black boxes. Just so people would think it was the asteroid that uncovered them. But all along, the so-called aliens had been set up and waiting. The Science Agency had been tracking the asteroid and knew when it would hit."

"What?"

"It's in the e-mail Tyce sent me."

That was true. Rawling and Dad had come up with the theory, hoping it had enough truth in it to be able to bluff Steven into admitting more. I'd sent it to Ashley by e-mail so she could be ready for this meeting.

"That's the most outrageous thing I've heard. Tyce is a space hero. I know you miss him badly, but you shouldn't make things up."

"You see," Ashley continued calmly, "when the dome was first established over 14 years ago, those black boxes were buried by someone on a secret mission from the dome. They were left there for an emergency."

"I've had enough out of you." Director Steven tried to look angry, but he couldn't quite pull it off. He seemed worried, and he looked around a few times as though he wondered if anyone was overhearing this.

"It was planned for the day or two before people on Earth who were part of the United Nations would have to decide whether or not to continue funding the dome. Fake aliens and fake antigravity and fake perpetual motion. If people believed in it, they wouldn't care how much was spent to keep the Mars Project going."

"All of this is in your e-mail?"

It was. Rawling and Dad had had a lot of time to think this through—ever since the explosion that was supposed to kill us. Those boxes were set up to *look* very convincing. But if the stuff inside could have been examined, it could easily have been seen as fake. We were convinced that was the reason everything was rigged to blow up.

The revolving globe? We'd guessed that, with electromagnetics from an energy source hidden underneath the box, triggered by the opening of the door, a globe would float, repelled by magnetics. Which was why the robot had short-circuited once the arm reached inside and touched the invisible currents.

"And more," Ashley said, plunging ahead and playing her role perfectly. "Tyce wrote that once the digital video scan had been made, someone here at the dome triggered devices to destroy all the alien artifacts. Because if anyone examined the aliens or the antigravity device, everybody would know they were fakes. But if video was all that remained, no one could dispute it."

"Someone at the dome?" he asked, worry in his voice.

Someone, I thought, *who at first insisted on reports every*

*six hours but then kept contacting us every hour. Someone
who had been speaking to Rawling on the radio while Dad
and I were down at the black boxes, showing Rawling the
aliens on the monitor. Someone who had heard all about it
from Rawling as it happened. Someone who waited until
the video feed had been beamed back to the dome by satellite
and then . . .*

"Yes," Ashley told Director Steven. Her face was con-
cerned. "Someone who then triggered a bomb to destroy the
platform buggy. That explosion wasn't an accident. It was
on purpose. Someone here at the dome wanted to kill the
only witnesses to the fake aliens. With them dead, only the
video would remain. People on Earth would fund the dome
for another hundred years, hoping to find the secrets behind
antigravity or perpetual motion. Secrets that don't exist."

Director Steven ran his hands wildly through his hair.
He glanced in all directions, then gave Ashley his attention. "And you have all this on e-mail? From Tyce? He sent it
before the explosion?"

"It's on my computer," Ashley said, ignoring the question
about the explosion.

"Has anyone else seen it?"

"No," she said. "I thought I should let you be the first to
know."

"No one else has seen it."

"I just told you that."

"I needed to be sure," Director Steven said. "Thank you."

"You're welcome. Are you going to find out who triggered the devices? Are you going to tell people the aliens were fakes, planted by an Earth mission?"

"Let's go for a walk," Director Steven answered.

"Walk?"

With a sudden movement, he grabbed Ashley's wrist and pulled her to her feet. Then he tightened his arm around her waist and clamped a hand over her mouth so she couldn't scream.

"A long walk," he said in a menacing tone. "Out on the surface of the planet."

CHAPTER 23

I'd been waiting for this moment.

In the robot body, I rolled out from behind the plants that had kept me hidden from Director Steven. With his back to me and one arm wrapped around Ashley's waist, he didn't see me coming. So I reached out and grabbed his wrist with titanium fingers. I locked my grip.

"Let her go," I demanded.

Director Steven found himself looking straight into my front video lens. His eyes bulged with surprise. Not at my appearance, though that would have surprised most people. No, Director Steven knew what the robot body looked like. That's not what surprised him.

"Impossible," he said. He had to know as soon as he saw the robot body that we hadn't been blown up.

"Not impossible," I said through the robot's voice box. "Dad and Rawling are in the platform buggy about five miles from here, where they are letting me control this robot body. Now let her go."

I tightened my grip. The titanium fingers of the robot body were capable of bending bars of steel. He screamed in pain. I lessened the grip slightly but did not release his arm. "Let her go."

Reluctantly, he did.

"It was you," I said. "Someone high up in the Science Agency on Earth is in on it too, right? So you were placed back as director?"

"This is insane," he protested.

Ashley backed away from Director Steven. Her face was not afraid but angry. "Jerk!" she said to him. She kicked him in the shins, then sat down on the bench.

"It is not insane." I held out my other hand. "Recognize this?"

Director Steven drew in a big breath of surprise. He tried to pull himself out of my grip.

"So you do recognize it," I said.

I held a small, gray, plastic box, with what looked like antennae sticking out of the sides. It was the same box we'd pulled off the axle of the platform buggy. Filled with high-powered explosives, it was just like the one on the video that had exploded the black boxes.

"Take it outside," Director Steven said, his eyes wide as he stared at it in my hand.

"Outside? Why?"

After I'd seen the little box on the monitor and remembered the one on the axle, Dad and Rawling had gone out of the platform buggy to remove the box. They'd taken the cover off but left the explosives intact, with the antennae in place. We'd driven safely away, leaving the explosives near the base of a hill. It hadn't surprised us when it blew only 15 minutes later, taking much of the hillside with it, leaving people at the dome with the mistaken impression that we'd died. And that's when Rawling and Dad had come up with their theory.

"Just take it outside!" Director Steven was frantic. "The whole dome could be destroyed!"

But a theory was only a theory unless it could be proved. Rawling had reassembled the cover of the gray box and inserted wires that would look like antennae. But only in dim lighting. Like right here and right now.

"Destroyed?" I said. "Are you suggesting this thing in my hand is a bomb? But how could you know, unless you were the person behind this?"

"No! No!" Director Steven finally realized what he might have admitted.

"Well," I said, "if it is *not* a bomb, we have nothing to worry about. Why not go for a ride in the other platform buggy? Just you and me. Once outside the dome, we will see if it is an explosive or not. How does that sound?"

"No!"

If the bomb went off, Director Steven realized he'd be the only one hurt. I, after all, was controlling the robot body. If it was destroyed, it wouldn't harm me.

"No? You do not want to go for a ride? Because maybe you know what this is?"

"Yes," he said. "I do. Let go of me, and I'll tell you everything."

I let go of his arm.

He backed away from me. He grinned. "I'm going to go get security. They'll take you away. And Ashley. When I erase her computer files, it will be your word against mine."

"The explosive," I said.

"I doubt very much you'll do anything with it here. In the dome? Where it will kill Ashley and your mother and everyone else?" Another grin of victory. "Fool." He turned and ran before I could stop him.

I rolled my robot body around to face Ashley.

She was frowning. "That didn't work exactly like you planned."

"Are you kidding?" I pointed at my video lens. "From the moment he got here, I recorded every word."

CHAPTER 24

08.06.2039

I don't really want to be sitting here in front of my computer. It's early evening, and I want to leave my minidome and go up to the telescope. But I know I'd better put the rest of what happened into my journal while it's still fresh in my head.

Rawling and Dad had guessed right. That's why we'd taken so many hours to return to the dome. They'd spent a lot of time throwing ideas back and forth until they'd realized exactly why and how all of it must have happened.

The entire alien thing was fake. It had been set up secretly right when the dome was first established. Director Steven had been part of it from the beginning. All those years ago Science Agency techies on Earth had made those fakes. And just to show how coldly careful the Science Agency had been, they'd used two techies who were battling terminal cancer, knowing that when they died they'd take their secret with them. The Science Agency had even planned the "alien discovery" by projecting which asteroid would hit 15 years later, because even back then the science committee knew the Mars Project funding would come up for review around that time.

Why go to so much effort for something fake?

How about $200 billion a year? That's what the Mars Project needs. And that's what it was going to get for another 10 years when the videos arrived at the United Nations budget committee by digital satellite . . . just in the nick of time to get every-body excited about aliens and new technology. Let's see . . . that's a total of $2 trillion. Not bad for a fake setup. And a couple of murders, if it had worked.

Director Blaine Steven . . .

I stopped keyboarding as a familiar chime on my computer alerted me to a new text message via IM. I saved my journal writing but didn't close the program, then clicked on my IM alert.

Tyce,

Are you going to meet me tonight? I want to talk.

I smiled and sent Ashley a message.

Talk? How about up at the telescope?

Seconds later, she wrote back.

Sounds good. How about I stop by and we'll go together? I'll bring Flip and Flop. They've been restless. I think they miss you!

I smiled again.

Come on over. And bring the koalas. I miss them too.

I sent the message, then returned to my journal.

> Director Steven heard about our planned trip from one of his techie moles—someone who spied for him and kept him informed of things happening at the dome. It was a techie whose job was to help prepare the platform buggies for field trips. This techie planted the bomb.

After we left the dome, this same techie helped ex-Director Steven send a coded message to the higher-ups in the Science Agency who had helped him set up this plan many years ago, while Steven was still on Earth. They pulled the strings to get Steven put in place as dome director again. From there, all that Director Steven needed to do was monitor our progress. As soon as he received the digital video scans, it served his purposes to get rid of the only witnesses to the fake aliens.

But now Steven is back under guard, along with the techie who helped him. They'll be going back to Earth on the next shuttle to face criminal charges there.

As for the funding, the funny part is this: it went through without the alien report. Members of the budget committee didn't even hear about the aliens. With a 7-5 vote in favor of budgeting more money, they decided to keep the dome going simply because it truly was important to Earth. Although Steven had sent the digital video scans back to Earth by satellite transmission, Dad and Rawling followed them up with the whole report about fakes. The Science Agency kept all of this out of the public news and is now investigating who else was involved.

Yet without a flat tire, it would have turned

out much differently. I shiver when I think of what would have happened to Dad and Rawling and me out on the surface of Mars if I hadn't seen that small gray box.

But all thoughts about death are scary. I can understand why people would rather listen to music or watch television or play computer games or do anything else to distract themselves from wondering about death. Because then you have to ask questions about God and why we're here and how the universe started and . . .

I stopped keyboarding. And smiled again. Tonight I'd be happy to talk about all of this with Ashley. It was great having a friend my age.

I heard her voice as she called out for me and then Mom's voice as she told Ashley I was in my room. I saved my writing, shut down my computer, and turned my wheelchair around so I was facing her when she entered.

"Hey," I said. "You got here fast."

"I ran," Ashley said. "I've got some news. You've got to promise to keep it secret. At least until my father announces it officially."

"Sure."

She stepped closer and whispered, "Interested in going to Jupiter?"

JOURNAL TWO

CHAPTER 1

Ambush!

Rawling McTigre, the director of the Mars Project, had warned me that, on this practice run in the Hammerhead space torpedo, I wouldn't be alone in the black emptiness 3,500 miles above the planet. But I'd already circled Phobos, one of the Martian moons, twice and seen nothing, so it was a complete surprise when my heat radar buzzed with movement from below.

Actually, it's wrong to say I had seen nothing. What I'd really seen was the silver glint of sunlight bouncing off Phobos. To do that, I'd raced at the moon with the sun behind me. At the speed I moved in the Hammerhead, the moon was almost invisible coming from any other angle. It was so tiny, and the backdrop of deep space so totally dark, except for the pinpoints of stars.

Without the sun at my back, straining for visual contact with Phobos was like trying to see a black marble hanging in front of a black velvet curtain.

It was also wrong to say the movement came from below.

In space, there *is* no up and down. It's difficult, though, not to think that way because I'm so used to living in gravity, weak as it is on Mars. So I thought of the Hammerhead's stabilizer fin as the top.

When the movement came from the belly side of the space torpedo, my mind instinctively told me it was below. Just like my mind instinctively told me to roll the Hammerhead away from the movement.

In one way, rolling my space torpedo was as easy as thinking it should roll. It's similar to how you move your arms or your legs. Your brain wills it to happen, and the wiring of your nervous system sends a message to your muscles. Then chemical reactions take place in your muscles' cells and they burn fuel, causing you to move.

It was the same way with the Hammerhead. My mind, connected to the computer, willed it to roll and it obeyed instantly. But it was really the computer on board that did all the hard work. It ignited a series of small flares along the stabilizer nozzles, allowing the torpedo to react as though it were flying through the friction of an atmosphere, not the vacuum of outer space.

I rolled hard to my right, then hard left, then downward

in a tight circle that brought the giant crescent of Mars into my visual.

The top of the massive red ball shimmered with an eerie whiteness, the thin layer of carbon dioxide that covered the planet. And behind it was the glow of the sun.

But I didn't have time to admire this beauty. The planet was getting closer—fast.

I told myself I wouldn't crash, that its closeness was just an illusion because it filled so much of my horizon. After all, the top of the Martian atmosphere was still over 3,000 miles away.

But I was moving at over four miles per second. That meant if I didn't change direction within the next 10 minutes, at this speed, I'd get fried to a crisp upon reentry.

I rolled upward, back toward Phobos, hoping to buy some time.

I didn't even bother trying to get a visual confirmation of my pursuer. Because of Rawling's earlier warning, I didn't need to see what was chasing me to know it was another space torpedo. This was the ultimate test of my pilot skills. Against another pilot.

I knew if I looked, I wouldn't be able to see the other space torpedo anyway. My Hammerhead was hardly longer and wider than a human body. Plus, space torpedoes are painted black, so they're almost impossible to detect visually in space from more than 100 yards away.

Right now, with the other pilot chasing me, I was locked in a whirling dance with another space torpedo 100 miles away, with both of us ducking and bobbing at around 15,000 miles per hour. Not even the best eyes in the universe would be able to watch this dogfight.

No, the only way I could detect the other space torpedo was with heat radar. Tiny as the vent flares were, the heat they produced showed up on radar like mushrooms as big as thunderstorms. Especially in the absolute cold of outer space.

That was good for me, being able to track the other space torpedo as easily as watching a storm cross the sky. But it also meant the pilot of the other torpedo could follow my movement.

And my Hammerhead was the lead torpedo, a sitting duck in the computer target sights of the pilot behind me.

I made a quick decision. I flared all of my vents equally for an instant. I knew my direction wouldn't change. But it would cause a big blast of heat, hopefully blinding the pilot behind me.

An instant later, I shut down all my vents, knowing my Hammerhead was now shooting through the mushroom of heat I'd just created.

I exited the other side of the heat mushroom with no power or flares to give away my presence. To the heat radar of the pilot behind me, my Hammerhead was as black and cold as outer space itself. I was now invisible.

I congratulated myself for my smart move.

Then I panicked. There was no heat mushroom on *my* radar either. The pilot behind me must have done the same thing—shut down all vent flares.

It could mean only one thing. The pilot had guessed my move and taken a directional reading of my flight path just before I shut down my vents.

I knew I was dead. Without vent flares to control the direction of my Hammerhead, I wouldn't be able to change direction until I reactivated them. It would take my computer 30 seconds to run through its preignition checklist. In space warfare, 30 seconds was eternity, because torpedo computers reacted much more quickly than human brains.

In 30 seconds, the computer of the torpedo behind me would figure out my line of travel and shoot me with a laser before I could reactivate and change direction.

Only 20 seconds left.

White flashed over my visual from the other torpedo's target scanner. I was dead center in the laser target controls.

I swallowed hard, preparing myself for the red killer flash that would follow in an instant, blowing my spacecraft to shreds. The explosion of my Hammerhead torpedo would be soundless since you can't hear screams in the vacuum of outer space.

Another white flash hit me instead.

I jumped. The target scanner behind me didn't need confirmation.

A third white flash.

There was still no red laser to superheat the fuel tanks and blow the Hammerhead apart.

I didn't understand. Three times I'd been right in the other pilot's sights. Why hadn't the other pilot fired the laser pulse?

Without warning, my vents reactivated at the 30-second mark. I rolled safely out of the way.

I looped, scanning my heat radar again to find the other space torpedo.

Then my visual and my consciousness melted into black nothingness.

CHAPTER 2

"I don't get it," I said to Rawling. "The pilot of the other space torp had me dead and let me go. What kind of computer program is that?"

A minute earlier the blackout of all my thoughts had signaled the end of my flight-simulator program. I was brought out of virtual reality and back to my body in a lab room under the dome.

I was still sweating from the effort, and my arm muscles shook from stress. I really looked forward to a glass of water.

Rawling leaned forward to unstrap me. Whenever I connected to the computer through virtual reality, my body was secured on a bed so I couldn't roll loose and break the connection.

"Could you be wrong, Tyce?" Rawling asked. "I know it's almost inconceivable that you might make a mistake, but . . ."

"Hah-ha," I said.

Rawling scratched his hair and smiled, the way he always did when he teased me. Over the last month, we had gone beyond the robot body I had learned to control. Rawling was supervising me as I learned the controls of a space torpedo we had nicknamed Hammerhead because it looked so much like the shark I'd seen on Earth DVD-gigaroms.

"Do you think that's been programmed?" I asked. "For the other pilot to show mercy?"

"That would surprise me. Mercy is something human." Rawling helped me sit up, then handed me a glass of water. He knew I always needed it badly when I exited virtual reality. "You were in a flight-simulation program. The other pilot was simply computer generated. It's not like there was another human linked into the program."

"It's also human to guess about my heat-vent trick. Which it did. Which in theory it's not supposed to do."

Instead of asking me what I meant, Rawling raised an eyebrow, something I practiced myself when I knew people weren't looking.

"Heat-vent trick," I repeated, still sitting on the bed and facing him. I drank deeply from the water before I continued. "At the beginning of the week, when you told me I had only a few days left to get ready for an enemy pilot, I planned to try the heat-vent trick during this flight simulation."

That wasn't quite true. I hadn't planned this trick all by

myself. I'd talked to Ashley about it, and together we'd come up with the idea.

"It's a way to make a light explosion in the enemy pilot's radar," I continued. "Then you coast out of the back side of it with so little power that you can't be tracked by heat radar."

Next I explained to Rawling how I had done it.

"Pretty good," he said, nodding enthusiastically. "Except for the 30 seconds you had to wait to reignite the stabilizer vents and get directional power again. I'm very, very surprised that the computer program was able to make an adjustment to let the pilot track you. So let me say this again. Maybe it was a mistake, you thinking you were in the target scanner. I mean, according to this program, the enemy pilot is supposed to destroy you at the first opportunity."

"Sure," I said, not convinced. I'd been flashed three times with the target scanner's white laser beam. Maybe once was my imagination but not three times. Was it possible the other pilot had given me three chances instead of blowing me away at the first opportunity? If so, the enemy pilot sounded too human to be computer generated.

Rawling helped me from the bed and into my wheelchair.

"I have a couple of questions," I said. With my hands, I rocked the wheels back and forth. It was something I did when I was restless, like other people might tap their fingers.

"Fire away," he said with a grin, like he knew it was a pun on the space-torpedo program I'd just gone through.

"Why a space torpedo?" I asked. "Don't get me wrong. After all those years of working with a robot, this Hammerhead is a lot of fun. And you know I love being in outer space, even if it's just virtual reality. Only . . ."

"Only what?"

"It seems a waste."

"Waste?" Rawling repeated.

"I know these virtual-reality computer training programs cost millions and millions of dollars to develop," I said. "So why would the government spend all this money to train anyone to fly something that doesn't exist?"

Rawling walked past me and shut the door. Then he spoke so quietly that I could barely hear him. "I guess now is as good a time as any to tell you. . . . Remember when the last shuttle arrived?"

Of course I did. Shuttles arrived from Earth only every three years. They were the lifeblood of the Mars Project, bringing new scientists and technicians and supplies, then returning to Earth with the scientists and techies who had finished their duty. As if that wasn't enough reason for me to remember, my dad was a space pilot, and he'd returned to Mars with the last shuttle. After getting to know him all over again, I'd finally started to like having him around.

"The Hammerhead does exist, Tyce," Rawling said. "And it arrived with that last shuttle."

"What! There really is a Hammerhead?" This was great. I could go into space. I could fly at speeds that no human ever flew. I could—

"Don't get too excited." He spoke so sharply that I blinked. "Sorry." He sighed. "The responsibilities that come with being director sometimes . . ."

I waited for him to finish. Suddenly the lines in his face seemed much deeper, and I saw a thicker streak of gray in his hair.

"Tyce, if you don't learn to fly the Hammerhead like it's part of your body, there's a good chance the dome won't exist in another few months."

CHAPTER 3

09.15.2039

Computer notes, I guess, are the only journal I, Tyce Sanders, have. It's a habit I started a few
months ago when it looked like the dome was running out of oxygen. I've found that writing into my
computer is a great way to sort out my thoughts.

And right now, after what Rawling explained to
me, I have plenty to sort out.

It's about a comet. A giant killer comet.

Rawling gave me the rundown. Far beyond the
solar system, thousands, millions, or maybe even
trillions of comets circle our sun in orbits that take
them hundreds or thousands of years. They lurk
out in the darkness, invisible becausee they are too

far away for the sun to warm them. Every once in a while, the gravity of a nearby star will nudge them out of their orbit, sending them into the outer edges of the solar system. If Jupiter's massive gravity pulls them closer, their orbit swings them toward the sun. That means the comet will then pass the inner planets of Mars, Earth, Venus, and Mercury. Sometimes the comet will hit the sun directly, blooming in incredible cosmic fireworks. Most of the time the comet flashes past the sun and heads back out to the darkness of the outer solar system, never to be seen again. But if its orbit has been changed enough, it will return again and again and again, like Halley's comet, which passes by the Earth every 76 years.

Comets are made of three parts. The heart is a big chunk of rock and ice. Picture a big black potato, hundreds of feet wide or up to 15 miles across. The coma is the sphere of gas and dust that surrounds the rock. And following behind is the tail—ice and dust released by the sun's heat. Even though a comet might be only a couple of miles wide, its tail can grow into a stream in the solar wind as long as a hundred million miles, reflecting the light of the sun in a dazzling display. It's the tail of the comet that's so beautiful.

And, like with humans, it's the heart that's so dangerous.

Look at it this way. Comets travel at 150,000 miles per hour. Even a small chunk of rock—say half the size of a football field—can make a crater a mile wide if it hits a planet. All it would take is the impact of a comet a couple of miles wide to destroy all life on Earth.

The comet Rawling was talking about was 12 miles wide. It—

"Hello, Mr. Sanders. Hello, Mrs. Sanders."

I knew that voice.

"Hello, Ashley," Mom answered. "Tyce is at his computer. Go on in."

Which meant Ashley would be at my door in a few seconds. I swung my wheelchair away from the computer and toward the door.

"Hello, Tyce," Ashley said from the doorway with her usual big grin.

"Hey," I said. She and I usually went up to the dome telescope after supper. But the telescope had been malfunctioning for the last couple of weeks, and the techie in charge hadn't been able to fix it yet. Just as well. The last thing I wanted was to look for a tiny bullet of deadly light that would show the comet getting closer to Mars by 150,000 miles every hour.

"Hey, back," Ashley said. Then she frowned. "What's wrong?"

"Nothing."

"Give me a break," she said. "I can tell when something's bothering you."

She pulled up a chair so we were facing each other. It hadn't taken Ashley long to get used to the fact that I was in a wheelchair. "Well, talk to me."

"If an asteroid was going to hit a planet, how would you stop it?"

She laughed. "That is so 20th century. I mean, all you need to do is watch some of those ancient premillennium movies where everyone on Earth is doomed because of a giant asteroid."

"And?" I insisted.

"The solution is so simple I can't believe you're asking. Attach a rocket engine to the asteroid and change its orbit. Alter it by a degree or two, and it misses the planet. Or blow it apart with a nuclear weapon. People stopped worrying about asteroids hitting the Earth long before we were born."

Seeing my face, Ashley stopped laughing. "Tyce, you still look worried."

Rawling was going to make the announcement the next morning, and I'd already told Mom and Dad at supper, so it was all right to discuss it with Ashley. She knew I worked with the robot and would find it interesting that now I was learning to fly a space torpedo.

"What if the asteroid broke up into hundreds of smaller pieces before you could divert it?" I asked. "What if any of those pieces was big enough to destroy this entire dome? And what if all of those hundreds of pieces were only two months away from hitting us?"

"Then," she said with total seriousness, "I would start to pray. Very hard."

"You can start tonight," I said.

Ashley inhaled sharply.

Then I told her what Rawling had explained to me. Back in 1994, a comet named Shoemaker-Levy 9 appeared from out of the darkness beyond the solar system, like some sort of prehistoric shark cruising up from the unexplored depths of the ocean. Jupiter's massive gravity pulled Shoemaker-Levy 9 closer and closer, and the comet crumpled. Splitting into 20 pieces, it slammed into Jupiter's upper atmosphere. Each explosion released the energy of a gigantic nuclear bomb, and it took over a year for the black clouds of the explosion to disappear from the telescopes aimed at Jupiter from Earth.

Now another comet was headed our way, like a lone black rocket of death. From what we were told by the Earth scientists, they expected this one, too, to break up as it passed Jupiter. The pieces, however, would miss Jupiter completely this time—and intercept Mars a few months later.

Unlike Jupiter, Mars has no atmosphere thousands of miles high to absorb the chunks of comet. Compared to Jupiter, Mars is the size of a marble. If only a few of those pieces hit anywhere on the planet, the impact would destroy the dome. If all those pieces hit, it could shatter the planet completely, sending a shock wave into the inner solar system. And with chunks of Mars flying in all directions, there was a big, big possibility that the Earth would be hit several months later by debris.

Rawling said it was my job to stop the comet before it stopped us.

CHAPTER 4

"Today's a workday," Rawling said. "Try to make it as short as possible. We want you in the virtual Hammerhead for at least a couple of hours."

I was back in the lab again. Earlier than usual. Considering how important it was for me to fly a Hammerhead in space, Mom and Dad and Rawling had agreed that my schoolwork could be put aside for now.

"Work?" I said. "I was hoping to see the actual Hammerhead. You know, for inspiration."

"Work," Rawling said firmly. "We want you to try something on the dome telescope. Blowing sand out of some rotational gears. I'm hoping that's the problem. We need the telescope operational to allow us to track the pieces of comet as it gets closer. Right now we're going blindly on the advice of Earth scientists who have to watch it from 50 million miles farther away. We can't afford to make any errors as we track the pieces of comet. Last time we did that kind of maintenance we had to send techies up in space suits. Not only did it take them hours, it was dangerous work up there. You, on the other hand . . ."

"Rawling, I thought the purpose of all this was to be able to explore the universe. You know, go boldly with a robot where no man has gone before."

"That too," he said. "Just not now. If you want to feel good about this kind of work, think of what the robot body cost the space program. That makes your boring maintenance work worth millions of dollars per hour."

Rawling helped me out of my wheelchair and onto the narrow medical bed. Then he began to strap me in place. What used to be exciting was now routine.

"For all those millions per hour, you want me to climb the ladder outside the dome?" I asked Rawling.

"Right. Techies have already set up the robot with a backpack and compressed air tank. All you have to do is blow sand out of the exposed gears. Shouldn't take much more than five minutes. Then you can get back to the Hammerhead virtual-reality program. The sooner you've got the training in, the sooner we can get you into space."

That was a good incentive. A very good incentive.

I nodded. "Checklist."

"Checklist," Rawling replied.

"First," I said, "no robot contact with any electrical sources."

"Check."

After all, my spinal nerves were attached to the plug. Any electrical current going into or through the robot could do serious damage to the robot—and to my own brain.

Rawling snugged down the straps across my stomach and chest to keep me from moving and disengaging the plug.

"Second," I said, continuing the list, "I disengage instantly at the first warning of any damage to the robot's computer drive." All I needed to do to disengage was mentally shout the word *Stop!*

"Check." Rawling placed a blindfold over my eyes and strapped my head in position. While I controlled the robot body, it was important for me not to be distracted.

"The robot is at the dome entrance?" I asked.

"Outside the dome entrance. The techies moved it there already to save you the time of clearing the double entrance. And when you're finished, leave it out there too. The techies will move it back in. That should save you 10 minutes in each direction and give you an extra 20 minutes on the Hammerhead program."

"Robot battery at full power?"

"Yes."

"Unplugged from all sources of electrical power?"

I already knew the answer. So did Rawling. If the robot was outside the dome, it was definitely unplugged. But Rawling was very strict about going through the entire checklist.

"Unplugged," he answered.

"I guess we're ready, then," I said. "If I have any other questions, I'll radio them in to you from the top of the dome."

"Checklist complete," Rawling said. He placed ear protectors on me as the last step. I was soundproofed and ready to go. I waited.

By now the sensation was familiar. In the darkness and silence of entering the robot computer, it felt like I was falling off a high, invisible cliff into a deep, invisible hole.

I kept falling and falling and falling. . . .

CHAPTER 5

When my imaginary fall ended, I was on the surface of the planet Mars.

Although my body was still strapped on a narrow bed in the dome laboratory, all the sensations reaching my brain through the robot told me I was on the planet's surface.

I love controlling this robot body. While my own body is in a wheelchair, this robot gives me the sensation of more freedom than any other human has experienced.

Except today wasn't Mars exploration but maintenance work.

I still didn't mind.

It beat sitting in a wheelchair.

I brought both the robot's titanium hands up in front of

a video lens and flexed the fingers, wiggling them to make sure everything worked properly.

I switched to the rear video lens. As promised, the compressed air backpack was in place.

I rolled forward to circle the dome.

Ashley has told me that the sky on Earth is blue and the sun is yellow but too bright to look at for more than an instant. She told me clouds are white or, if they hold rain, gray. She said when the sun rises or sets, it stays the same color, but the clouds might turn pink or red or orange or a mixture of all those colors.

On Mars, when the sun rises, it is blue against a butterscotch-colored sky.

A few hours had passed since sunrise, and now the sky was red because sunlight scattered through dust particles at a different angle. At sunrise, it had been about minus 100 degrees Fahrenheit. Now it was 50 degrees above zero. Mars has such radical daily temperature differences because the atmosphere is too thin to hold heat. As soon as the sun set at the end of the day, the planet's heat would bleed back into the cold of outer space.

The 40-mile-an-hour wind and the sand it threw at my titanium shell didn't bother me. With such little atmosphere, even strong winds don't have the force they would on Earth. And the robot body, about the size of a man, was built so tough that it would be standing long after human bodies fell.

I reached the ladder to the dome. Without hesitation, I grabbed one rung with the titanium fingers of my right hand and pulled, holding the entire weight of the robot with one arm. I reached for the next rung with my left hand. One hand after another, I climbed quickly, robot wheels bouncing against the ladder. My arms had such strength that I didn't need to support myself with legs.

It took less than a minute to get to the top of the dome. I dragged myself onto the platform surrounding the telescope lens.

From there I had an incredible view. I saw the dome's greenhouse about a half mile away, where scientists were trying to raise plants that would grow on the planet's surface. As I scanned the horizon, the red mountains, and the brownish red sand of the valley plains, movement on the other side of the greenhouse caught my attention.

Movement?

It was far too small to be a platform buggy on an expedition. Unless it was a techie or a scientist in a space suit, there should be nothing moving out there except sand shifted by the wind.

I clicked my forward video lens to get a close-up and nearly jumped out of my robot's titanium shell.

It was another robot. Making circles in the sand.

Impossible.

CHAPTER 6

"Rawling." My voice sounded mechanical since it traveled through a sound-activated communication device attached to the robot body.

"Tyce. You're at the telescope. Need more instructions?" Rawling asked.

I swiveled the robot video lens. The part of the telescope that extended from the dome observatory was like a short tube, twice as wide as the robot's outstretched arms. It rotated on a track railing. Spraying compressed air into the rotational gears would be a simple task.

"No," I said. "Yes."

"No? Yes? Make sense, Tyce."

"No, I do not need instructions on how to clean the gears. Yes, I need advice."

"On what?"

"I am going to switch one of my lenses to the video screen in the lab. You tell me what you see."

"Sure."

I made the switch. I zoomed in even closer and waited for Rawling. What he would see was a robot body like mine but different.

Rawling's whistle of surprise broke the silence around me. "If I didn't know better, I'd say it was a robot." His voice, though still calm, was louder in the communication device.

"Me too. And one sleeker than mine."

The robot body I controlled looked bare bones compared to this new one, whose legs, arms, and fingers were sheathed with shiny silver, like metallic skin.

"Tyce," Rawling said into the speakers, "it looks to me like a second-generation robot."

"My guess too," I said. I paused. I didn't want to ask Rawling this question. But I had to do it. "Have you been keeping a secret from me?"

"No," he said a second later. "And as dome director, I should know about this. Which means someone somewhere has been keeping it secret from both of us."

"That's not good, is it?"

Rawling knew what I meant. The former director of the dome, Blaine Steven, had kept too many secrets. I couldn't forget that the last secret he kept nearly killed

Rawling and me and my dad during our expedition across the planet.

"No," he said, "that's not good at all."

"Should I try to catch that robot?" I asked.

"Finish your telescope maintenance and get back down as soon as you can."

"But—"

"I'll explain why when you return."

CHAPTER 7

"Tyce, I've pulled up on the computer screen the last 48 hours of activity at the dome entrance."

We had finished three hours of training on the Hammerhead virtual-reality program, and I now sat in Rawling's office. "So who moved that other robot out there?" I asked. It would definitely show on the activity record. There was no other way in or out of the dome.

"Look for yourself." Rawling turned the computer screen my direction.

Digital images of the dome entrance flashed in front of me. It was like entering an igloo with two sealed doors. The outer door remained sealed when the inner door opened. Once the people or cargo moved into the entrance area, the inner door closed and sealed before the outer door opened so oxygen wouldn't leak out and the dome's pressure wouldn't change. It was a 10-minute process and so important that the entrance was under computerized surveillance all the time.

I kept watching the computer screen. In the lower right-hand corner, digital numbers flicked, recording the time. Rawling was fast-forwarding the images so quickly that in less than five minutes, I saw all 48 hours.

"The only robot going outside is mine," I said.

"Exactly. Which is very disturbing. What does that tell you?"

I thought it through before I answered. "The robot has been outside longer than 48 hours. Which means if it has been used at all, it should need recharging. But the only source of charging is inside the dome. So either it hasn't been used much, or it doesn't need recharging."

Rawling nodded. "What really scares me is that I reviewed the dome entrance surveillance discs as far back as they go. One month. That robot did not enter or leave the dome in the entire time. So it's been out beyond the greenhouse, hidden from anyone in the dome for at least a month. And I'd be surprised if today was the only time that robot was active."

"Surprised?" I asked.

"You saw what the other robot was doing. Practice activities. Lifting. Circling. Digging. Practice is just that. Practice. Repeated activities. So what are the chances that the only time someone activated it was while you were on top of the dome?"

"Slim. It would have to be a big coincidence."

"No one but you and I and two techies knew you were going up there for maintenance work today. The top of the dome is probably the only place that would give anyone the chance to see the robot. So whoever practices it would have felt safe to use it. I'd say it's much more likely that the robot has been used often and daily." Rawling rubbed his chin. "And that tells us . . ."

I thought again. "First of all, someone else in the dome is running a robot. And second, either the robot has an incredible battery power that doesn't need charging very often, or it has a way of replenishing its power outside the dome."

"Yes and yes," he said. "But it's something even bigger that bothers me the most."

I knew the answer to that. "You're the director, and you don't know about it."

"Unfortunately, you're right again."

That's why Rawling had told me to finish the telescope maintenance and return to the dome as if we hadn't seen the other robot. Rawling wanted the chance to search for whoever controlled it without that person knowing Rawling was in the middle of a search.

"Think about what's been happening in the last few months." Rawling listed the major events since I'd learned to control the robot body. During an oxygen crisis, the former director had tried to save a select few scientists, keeping it secret from the other 180 people under the dome, whom he was willing to let die. Later we'd discovered that the director had hidden oxygen tanks to help save hybrid animals bred through illegal genetic experiments, rather than saving the 180 dome residents. And recently, the revealing of a falsified ancient alien civilization had proved there was a conspiracy between a group of dome officials on Mars and a government group on Earth.

"What do all of these have in common?" Rawling asked. He answered his own question. "Secrecy, conspiracy, and ulterior motives at top levels." He shook his head. "I came here as a medical doctor. I was willing to give up 10 or 15 years of my life because I believed—and still believe—that the Mars Project can save millions of Earth lives."

I nodded. I'd never witnessed the conditions on Earth myself, of course, but I'd been told they weren't the greatest. There was a threat of overpopulation, and governments were barely holding control as everyone fought for resources. The team's arrival on Mars was Phase 1 of a long-term plan to establish the dome. Phase 2, which my mom had already started, was genetically altering plants that could grow outside the dome so that more oxygen could be added to the atmosphere. The long-range plan—over a hundred years— was to make the entire planet a place for humans to live outside of the dome. If Mars could be made a new colony, then Earth could start shipping people here to live. If not, new wars might begin, and millions of people would die from war or starvation or disease.

"The hope that this dome represents," Rawling continued, "has been enough to keep most of the political powers on Earth working together. It's like a light at the end of the tunnel, even though it's far away and small. But from the few communications I've had, some political leaders on Earth are becoming less willing to work together. So there's a good chance war might break out there soon." He paused and looked intently at me. "Since I've taken over as director, I've discovered that even though we are 50 million miles from Earth, the politics continue here."

Now I shook my head. "That doesn't make sense. I mean, if there is some sort of ongoing conspiracy here at the dome, with a secret circle of people among the scientists, why would the high-level Earth powers put you in the position of director? Wouldn't they want someone from the secret circle in power?"

"I've thought about this long and hard. I want to believe some of the high-level people on Earth don't know about the hidden circles here at the dome. And that the ones who *do* want me in position because then it will definitely appear there is no conspiracy. In the meantime, with enough scientists as part of the hidden circle, things can continue the way it used to be under the former director's control."

"Any use in asking him?"

Because of ex-director Blaine Steven's part in the oxygen crisis, then later in the ancient alien civilization hoax, he was in lockup, waiting to be sent back to Earth when the shuttle left again.

"No good at all," Rawling said with a tired smile. "All he has to do is deny any knowledge. And we have no proof."

"Except for the other robot. It didn't get here without someone pulling levers back on Earth."

"Bingo," he said.

"Bingo?"

"Sorry. It's an old Earth expression. A game people played when I was your age."

"What does this 'bingo' have to do with what I said?"

"*Bingo* means you won."

"I won?"

Rawling sighed. "Forget it. All I meant was that I think you're right. Someone pulled levers back on Earth to smuggle another robot out here. If I can find out who is behind the other robot, I might be able to learn more about the secret levels of power here at the dome. If we do that, I'll be able to figure out more about what's happening back on Earth."

He sighed again. "And there is that other matter. Remember? A comet that's about to shotgun Mars as target practice."

CHAPTER 8

That night, in the silence that usually fell beneath the dome after the supper hour, when the scientists and techies retreated into their minidomes to read e-books, I followed my own usual habit.

I wheeled across the dome, taking a path on the main level that wound between the dimmed minidomes, and headed to the telescope on the third level. Although I had gone there nearly every night since learning to handle the electronic controls of the telescope as a kid, on this night, like the night before, I didn't want to look through the telescope. To me, the approaching comet was an enemy. It was almost like if I ignored it, it might go away.

No, I had a different reason for going to the telescope.

And when I got there five minutes after leaving our minidome, that reason was there and waiting for me.

"Let me run an idea past you," I said to Ashley.

I sat near the eyepiece of the telescope. That was one handy thing about being in a wheelchair. You always had a place to sit.

"Sure," she said. She'd pulled up a small bench from the side of the platform and moved it beside me. We both stared downward at the quietness of the dome floor beneath us.

"Remember I've been telling you about the virtual-reality Hammerhead?"

"I'll bet you spent a lot of time today on it," she replied. "Especially after what Rawling announced to everyone at the meeting today."

Rawling had informed all the scientists and techies about the approaching comet, and then he had promised everyone there was nothing to worry about. He'd told them that a new space torpedo was being prepared to intercept and destroy the comet pieces long before they reached Mars. However, he hadn't told them I would be doing it—he didn't want the extra pressure on me. After all, I was still a kid, and lots of people under the dome still treated me that way.

"At least three hours. Much more than that and my brain gets too tired."

"Hard work, huh?"

"Hard work," I agreed. "At least today was just a practice run. Without an enemy pilot to face. But tomorrow . . ."

"Back into combat?"

"I know it's just virtual-reality combat, but it's still tough. That's why I want to run another idea past you."

"Which is . . . ?"

"I'm going to blow up a moon."

"What?" Ashley snapped her eyes onto mine.

"It's just virtual reality, remember? So I won't *really* be blowing up one of Mars's moons."

"But why?" She kept staring at me.

"Simple. I told you before that it's hard to stop in space. I mean, the Hammerhead goes about 15,000 miles an hour. Which means that once you're in front of the enemy space torpedo, you're in big trouble. You can't suddenly slow down and let the other torpedo go by. You stay out in front until finally you get blasted. Even if it is a virtual-reality blast."

"But blowing up a moon?"

"Last time that pilot seemed to come out of nowhere, but I think the space torpedo was hiding by hovering in one of the craters of Phobos. So here's my plan. I'll go past Phobos, just like before. When the torpedo comes out on my tail, I'm going to make a loop back toward the moon. And I'll blast Phobos apart. The lasers are supposed to be that powerful, and Phobos is not near as thick as it is wide. It should be no problem to knock Phobos into a dozen or so chunks."

"I don't get it," Ashley said. "You'll be out of laser power. You'll have nothing left to shoot the other torpedo."

"My gamble is that I won't need to. I should be able to fly through the hole I blast into Phobos. The enemy torpedo will be following so close behind that it's almost certain to get hit by one or more of the chunks of moon caused by the explosion." I shrugged. "It's not much of a gamble. I mean, once you're followed by a space torpedo, you're almost certain to get shot anyway. So why not try something totally unexpected?"

"Might work," she said. "Like you said, it's just a virtual-reality program. In real life you might not want to blow apart a moon."

"Real life," I echoed. "Not to change subjects, but can we talk about Earth?"

"You always want to talk about Earth." Ashley stood and began pacing the small platform of the telescope area.

"You put me off every time I ask. But this time I want to hear about where you grew up."

Stopping briefly, she tilted her body left, resting her right hand on her right hip. It was a trademark Ashley pose. "What matters is where I am now. Not what happened before. You know I don't like talking about my family life."

That was true. All Ashley had said was that her parents

had recently divorced. I didn't know why—it was one thing she found too painful to discuss. Her father was a scientist, and evidently so good that when he'd insisted he wouldn't visit Mars unless he was allowed to take Ashley, he was given permission. No other scientist in the history of the dome had been allowed that privilege.

"You don't have to tell me about your mother," I said. "That's not what I meant. Remember you told me that you grew up in a place called Denver, Colorado? And how you've told me about the mountains and the lakes?"

"I remember," Ashley said. "It's easy to miss all that when you're on Mars."

"How about if you were born on Mars and have never seen Earth in the first place?"

She smiled for an instant. "Good point."

"Anyway," I continued, "I was trying to learn more about Colorado and Denver, and I tried a search engine on the newspaper files loaded on the mainframe. You forgot to tell me about that tornado a few years back that took out a whole section of the city. That must have been something. I mean, I've read all I can about tornadoes, but I can't imagine what it would be like to go through one. Were you scared?"

"I wish we could talk about something else," Ashley said. It didn't surprise me. She never liked talking about her childhood or her family life.

"Sure," I said. "How about you talk. I'll just listen."

So she began to tell me about her homework assignments.

But I didn't really listen. I was thinking about the tornado that had never hit Denver. I had just made that up to see what she would say.

I wondered why she hadn't told me there was no tornado.

Which made me begin to wonder about a lot of other things.

CHAPTER 9

09.16.2039

Here I am, late at night, clicking my computer keyboard for this journal, when I should be sleeping. The thing is, thinking about the comet headed for Mars and the destruction it might cause has got me thinking other questions. Especially after I mentioned the tornado to Ashley.

I mean, tornadoes cause destruction too. Maybe not as much as chunks of comet crashing into a planet, but from what I've read about them, they are natural disasters that can hurt or kill hundreds of people at a time. Same with hurricanes, flash floods, earthquakes, monsoons, and even volcano eruptions.

Not long ago, because of the oxygen crisis and my mom's strength even in the face of death, I began to believe in the existence of God. And not only a God "out there" but a God who cares about me. You might find it strange, but that belief happened through science. The more I learned about the universe, the harder it was to believe that human life happened by accident. One scientist a long time ago said the chances of that were similar to the chances of blowing up a junkyard and having all the pieces fall together to form a perfectly running high-speed sports car. Lots of other scientists, like my mom and Rawling, agree. Because of all the details of the universe that had to happen the exact right way at the exact right time, the presence of human life "by accident" on the planet Earth would be like winning the same lottery every week in a row for a year. Pretty low chances.

When you start believing in a Creator and wondering if the universe was actually created for a reason, then you have to start wondering why even further.

And that's where I've been for the last few months. Wondering why—and trying to fit the pieces all together. Why would someone—who I'm now sure is God—create a universe and all of us in it? Didn't he have enough to do? Was he bored, so he decided to create us? Or did he do it because he had some big purpose in mind?

I've also come to believe that I have a soul—a part of me invisible to science and medicine. A part of me that longs for meaning. A part of me that feels love, happiness, hope, and sadness. When I realized I had a soul, I wondered why even further.

It's the why questions that can drive you nuts.

Like right now. Late at night. Here under the dome. In front of my computer.

If God made us, loves us, and gives us a soul, why do bad things like tornadoes and hurricanes and volcano eruptions happen to us? Is God a father who lets bad things into the house to hurt his kids—on purpose? Or does God still love us and yet allow bad things to happen sometimes? If so, why doesn't the bad stuff just happen to bad people, rather than good people? And good things just to good people?

Right now I'm staring at my computer screen, half wanting to smile and half wanting to hit my head against a wall.

It was a lot easier a few months ago when I didn't ask the why questions. Now I think about them constantly. Especially when it's quiet under the dome and an exploding comet is headed directly for Mars.

So I don't have any choice but to think about those questions.

I hope I get some sleep tonight.

CHAPTER 10

Hammerhead.

The real Hammerhead.

The next morning Rawling and I stood in front of a storage area near the back of the dome.

A middle-aged techie named John Chateau, a French-Canadian who liked to comb his gray hair over a big bald spot on the top of his head, had just opened the door for us.

"Incredible," I said.

The Hammerhead stood on tail fins in a tall, thin crate made of protective plastic tubes. It looked just like the virtual-reality one. The nose of it had flat, wide stabilizer fins that gave it the appearance of a hammerhead shark. Almost hidden at the edges of the stabilizer fins were the holes of dozens of tiny flare nozzles. On the back of the space torpedo, just like a shark fin, was another stabilizer with dozens more tiny flare nozzles. It was black, with the kind of paint that reflected no light. The Hammerhead was only about seven feet tall and maybe double the width of a human body. Just the size of a giant shark.

John nodded with enthusiasm. "Tell you what, kid, this storage area was declared off-limits to all techies. I didn't even know what was in here until yesterday. As a telescope man, I sure wish I could use this to go into outer space instead."

Rawling had explained to me that he didn't know the Hammerhead was at the dome until receiving an encrypted message from Earth a week earlier. In other words, it was just one more secret that Blaine Steven, the former director, had kept from the rest of us.

"It may look like a rocket ship, but it's the most sophisticated robot in the history of humankind," John said. He looked directly at me. "Computer-wise, it has all the functions of the robot you control. But what a difference in appearance, huh?"

"Incredible," I repeated.

"Let me tell you about this baby," John continued quickly, as if he were a little kid proud of his first go-cart. "Most space vehicles need huge rockets and thrusters to be able to escape the gravity of a planet. Huge rockets and thrusters need huge fuel tanks. Nearly 90 percent of the bulk of a vehicle is needed just for that. It doesn't leave much for the actual travel out in space."

John reached through the plastic slats and patted the

Hammerhead. "This baby is small enough that it is launched from space. Yep, we take it up in a shuttle. That means all of its fuel is there for space travel. And you notice how small it is. That's because it only has room for the onboard computers and one pilot in a space suit. Once again it cuts back the need for extra fuel. Think of it this way. No extra weight or waste is put into it for life support. The space suit already has it. A person can live three days on the surface of Mars in a space suit. So a person can live three days in this thing." He paused. "Of course, no one expects a pilot to be in there that long. The Hammerhead was built for high-speed missions. Like a race car, not a motor home."

"It will really go 15,000 miles an hour?" I asked.

"More. Far more." John sounded as proud of it as if he had designed it himself. "When you throw a rock here in the dome, it accelerates with the initial force. Then gravity and the friction of air slow it down. In space there's no gravity. No friction. If you throw a rock in space, it will never lose that initial acceleration. The nozzles of the Hammerhead are extremely efficient. They compress the fuel burning and create tremendous pushing power. Whatever force you apply with this in outer space keeps accelerating. Think of it like a rock that gains speed as you drop it from a tall building. Say you're already at 15,000 miles per hour. If you gun it with another burst of nozzle flares, it will accelerate another 15,000 miles per hour and keep that speed of 30,000 miles per hour."

"And so on?" I asked.

"Yep! There's nothing to slow it down, ever, except reverse nozzle thrusts. The only limitations you have are fuel limitations. I believe—" he cupped his face with his right hand and stared thoughtfully past Rawling and me— "if you accelerated this until all your fuel was gone, you'd be at roughly 1.5 million miles per hour." He laughed. "Not that anyone would ever want to do that. And, of course, you wouldn't be able to find a way to stop. Unless you ran into something."

Very funny, I thought. He wouldn't be the pilot. As Rawling had told me a dozen times, the Hammerhead had been designed to be flown by someone with virtual-reality skills and the bio-implant in the spine to translate those skills into actual flight. Even if I would be doing it by remote, running into something wasn't a pleasant thought.

"You are certainly knowledgeable about this," Rawling said to John. "Especially for someone who didn't even know about the existence of the Hammerhead until yesterday."

John beamed. "Thank you. It helped that I was able to spend most of last evening going through the technical manual on it. I'm going to be the one helping Dr. Jordan. He's the expert who helped design and test this back on Earth."

Dr. Jordan. Ashley's father. Strange that he'd kept this a secret so long. And that Ashley, if she did know about it, hadn't mentioned it to me.

Or maybe it wasn't so strange. She did seem secretive at times about anything that happened back on Earth.

But I didn't have time to chase those thoughts now.

"One thing," Rawling said thoughtfully. "You mentioned a pilot in a space suit. I understood from the Science Agency's last communication that Tyce would handle this the same way he handles the robot. By remote. Why would there be a need for a pilot on board?"

John frowned. "Then someone yanked your chain, Dr. McTigre. There's no possible way to pilot this except by having someone on board. I mean, the range of this ship far exceeds any remote. So what happens if the ship gets on the other side of a planet like Mars? No remote is going to be able to send or receive information."

"You're telling me," Rawling said, "that Tyce is actually going to be *inside* this space torpedo?"

"No other way," John answered. "Why did you think otherwise?"

"Dr. Jordan didn't once tell me that," Rawling said, angry. "He implied that Tyce would fly it the same way he handles the robot. It's one thing to let Tyce try new technology and another to make him a guinea pig."

"Look," John said, "Dr. Jordan headed a team of Earth scientists who designed this specifically for a pilot like Tyce. Now we're facing that killer comet. If Tyce doesn't fly it, who will? And if no one flies it, what happens to the dome?"

Rawling didn't say anything else. Because we all knew the answers—but didn't want to hear them.

Back in the lab, Rawling shook his head. "I don't know about this."

"Is there a choice?" I asked. "Would you rather I get killed in the dome when the comet pieces hit Mars? Or would you like to give me a chance to save myself and everyone else?"

"I don't know if there's a choice," he answered, "and I'm angry about it. I'm angry that no one told me about the comet until a week ago. I'm angry that no one told me that Dr. Jordan was part of this. I'm angry that until a week ago I didn't even know the Hammerhead existed under this dome." He rubbed his eyes. "And I'm angry that there's probably a hundred other things that have been kept from me." He gave me a tight smile. "I'm so angry now that I'm even more determined to stay as director and get to the bottom of all this."

"Good," I said.

I had some questions of my own, and I hoped they'd be answered during today's flight-simulation program.

Rawling stared off into space briefly, then sighed. "Well, let's get to business." He pushed me in my wheelchair over to the bed and lifted me onto it. "Virtual reality today. That's all. You're not really going to be in space. You're going to be part of a computer program test run. Remember that. Tonight we talk to your parents about the real thing."

Sure, I thought as he strapped me into position. *When we talk to my parents, they'll come to the same conclusion: as much as they hate the idea of putting my life in danger, there's really no choice. I'll have to go out into the space beyond Mars in a tube barely longer and wider than my body. A tube that travels up to 1.5 million miles per hour. If I mess up, everyone on Mars and maybe everyone on Earth will die. Talk about pressure.*

We went through the checklist without our usual joking around. Rawling adjusted the blindfold over my eyes and the headset over my ears.

Soon everything around me was dark. I was left alone with all my scary thoughts.

Somehow virtual reality wasn't fun anymore.

Then I began to fall and fall and fall into the deep, deep black. . . .

CHAPTER 11

Silence. Monstrously thick silence.

And no sense of motion.

Rawling has told me that on Earth, when you're in a car speeding down the highway, fence posts will snap past you, one by one, in a blur of speed that is both frightening and exciting. In space, however, the stars are at such vast distances that you can't judge your speed in relation to their movement. That's because there is none. Even the sun—a white, glaring ball of fire that looks like it's in your back pocket—is 150 million miles from Mars.

Even worse, you feel no sense of weight—except during acceleration or deceleration. When you are cruising at over 15,000 miles an hour, you feel nothing but the beating of your heart. All around you, it is velvety black, broken only by stars.

That kind of aloneness is frightening.

I switched from human visual and human audio to the onboard computer receptors.

In the blink of an eye, it seemed I had been thrown into a crazed pinball machine.

Heat radar showed an approaching space torpedo coming in from my lower right. That radar then coordinated with signals bounced off the face of Mars to give me speed and location readings. I was already at 30,000 miles per hour, with impact radar warning me of harmless space dust. Then a clanging alert told me Phobos was one minute away—only 500 miles.

So this is the situation I've been given in today's combat program, I thought, grinning. I had less than 30 seconds to make a decision.

But I'd already decided much earlier what I'd do. It was something I'd only talked about with Ashley.

I flashed the surface of Phobos with my locator laser. At 300 miles, the laser pocked the small moon like a white dart. Yet I knew that in the blackness of outer space, the white target circle would have appeared like a neon billboard to the other pilot in this flight simulation program.

Twenty seconds to impact.

I kept the white laser circle steady at the center of the moon. It was only 18 miles wide, but at 200 miles away, it was starting to fill my visual.

My impact radars went into high alert.

Fifteen seconds.

I held off on the red laser beam that would destroy the moon.

Twelve seconds.

Ten.

In the remaining eight seconds, I did something that takes far longer to describe than accomplish. I rolled the Hammerhead hard left, taking a line that would almost scrape the side of the moon with my space torpedo. I vented all my flares, then shut down. Just as I'd done the first time I'd taken the Hammerhead into virtual-reality combat.

A heat mushroom would have filled the other pilot's radar. And, just as before, I coasted out of that heat mushroom. Invisible and untrackable.

Only this time my own heat radar showed that the pilot had fallen for my trick. The heat tracks of the other torpedo had peeled off from Phobos and it had slowed, as if it were going to give Phobos a wide circle and wait for me to show up again.

I drifted for another 30 seconds. Right before peeling away from Phobos, I'd rolled hard enough so that my newly accelerated path would curve me back toward Mars. Actually, between Mars and the space torpedo that waited for me on the other side of Phobos.

That meant when I reignited, this time it would be me

behind the other torpedo. I'd be in a perfect position to chase and destroy it.

Which I did, firing my virtual-reality laser weapon with exact timing.

The heat mushroom of the exploding space torpedo seemed to fill my whole radar screen. Just like my smile filled my entire face.

CHAPTER 12

"Let me tell you what I don't like," my dad said with an edge to his tone.

Dad, Mom, Rawling, and I sat in the common area of our minidome. Rawling had just explained to them what we'd learned today about the Hammerhead. That it was actually real—and present on Mars.

"First, it bothers me that I piloted the shuttle here with a cargo list that was false," Dad continued, his dark blond hair waving angrily with each gesture. "Only someone high up in the Science Agency or the military on Earth would have the kind of pull to get away with that." He frowned, and his square face looked fierce. "I don't like being messed with by those clowns."

Mom smiled at him. "Honey, don't bottle up your emotions. It could give you ulcers."

While I didn't get my looks from her—she was tall and thin with dark hair and a beautiful face—I definitely got my sense of sarcasm from her.

Normally her teasing worked, and Dad lightened up. Tonight he ignored her comment. That's when I knew he was really bugged—and that he, too, believed some sort of conspiracy was going on.

"Second," Dad said, "I can't believe they shipped it here secretly just for the comet."

Rawling, always a good listener, leaned forward.

"For starters," Dad explained, "you know it takes eight months to get from Earth to here."

Yet the shuttles only arrived once every three years. The reason was that pilots had to wait until the planetary orbits were close together. Planned right, the trip was only 50 million miles. But if a ship left Mars just as Earth was headed to the opposite side of its orbit, the trip would take double the time. Much of the three-year trip meant waiting either on Earth or on Mars. Dad would be leaving again soon, and I wouldn't see him for another three years. It was something I didn't want to think about.

"What I want to know, then," Dad insisted, "is how the military people on Earth knew about the comet ahead of time. If I understand your explanations, Rawling, comets in the far reaches of the solar system are next to invisible until they get close to Saturn. At best, we have only two months' notice of its arrival beyond Mars. Yet the Hammerhead was sent on a shuttle nearly eight months ago. Did someone on Earth know 10 months ago that the comet would be a threat? If so, why wait this long to warn us? And why ship the Hammerhead secretly?"

"Maybe," Mom said, "the Science Agency authorities didn't want people on Earth to panic. From all the reports, things are politically unstable. Maybe news of a killer comet would upset the balance."

Mom and Dad both looked at Rawling.

"I'm afraid I can't answer those kinds of questions," he said. "Believe me, I'm as frustrated as you are. I'm director of this dome. I should know about everything. But I wasn't informed about the comet—or the Hammerhead—until last week when Tyce began his training on the computer program. Let me point out that it must have taken at least a couple of years on Earth for the scientists to develop the flight-simulation computer program and even more time to build the Hammerhead. My gut feeling is that once they knew Tyce's operation let him handle virtual reality directly through his nervous system, they began work on the Hammerhead. And that was when Tyce was only six or seven years old!"

Dad stood. He crossed his arms as he stared down at Rawling. "When they started this program is the least of my concerns. What I'm really worried about is how little training he'll get with the Hammerhead before he heads out into space in a cigar tube!"

Rawling stood too. He didn't back down from Dad's glare. "I care about Tyce as much as you do."

Mom got up quickly and pushed them apart. "Do you two have any idea what's happening here? You're both angry, and you're both looking to fight back against what's making you mad. Except you can't, because the people behind this aren't here. You two are friends. Don't let this destroy that. Especially when now is the time all of us have to work together."

Dad kept glaring at Rawling. "I'm not going to kiss and make up with someone that ugly."

Rawling glared back. "Think I'd let anyone with breath as bad as yours even get close?"

Then they both grinned.

Mom sighed. "Men." She sat beside me and rested her hand on my arm. I patted her hand.

"I'm learning fast, Dad," I said. "By the time the comet arrives in two months I don't think I'll have any problems with maneuvering the Hammerhead."

Now it was Rawling's turn to sigh. "This is the part I really hate to bring to all of you."

"Yes?" Mom's hand tightened on the muscles of my forearm.

"I just received another communication from Earth.

They say that the Hammerhead's weapon system is going to need testing. If we don't do it now, we won't know whether it'll be effective when the comet is near."

"So when is Tyce going up?" Dad demanded.

"Tomorrow," Rawling said. "A small asteroid is making a loop that will come within five million miles of Mars."

"Five million miles!" Mom exclaimed. "This isn't like sending someone to the store for milk and bread."

"No," Rawling answered. "It isn't. I wish I could see some way around it. But that asteroid is the only one that will be close enough in the next two months to test the Hammerhead."

He eyeballed Dad. "I'm hoping you can take Tyce into orbit sometime in the afternoon. He'll have to make his first real run in the Hammerhead then."

CHAPTER 13

Normally I was asleep by 11:00. Normally I'd read from an e-book until I fell asleep.

Normally, though, I wouldn't wake up the next day to face the prospect of buckling myself into a thin tube of metal and traveling a couple of million miles. Alone. In an experimental space vehicle.

And normally I wouldn't be filled with sadness and anger. But I couldn't help but go over it again and again. It seemed like my best friend had betrayed me. Who else but Ashley knew that I was going to go into the flight-simulation program and blow up the moon as a way to defeat the other pilot? Who else would have pulled away as I approached the moon?

But if it was Ashley, that led to a bunch of other questions. How had she become part of the flight simulation? Why keep it secret?

So I didn't sleep.

At two thirty in the morning, after staring at the ceiling of the minidome all night, I lifted myself out of bed and into my wheelchair.

I was restless. Too restless to go to my computer and make journal entries. I silently rolled out of my room, out of our minidome, and into the hush of the big dome. The only sound was the gentle, distant whoosh of the air circulation pumps. It was dim, with most of the lights turned down. All the other minidomes were in shadow.

I had to talk to Ashley, but I wondered if I'd have the courage to knock on her minidome when I got there. Especially at three in the morning.

I rolled forward farther in the silence and dimness.

Halfway to the other minidome, I heard a strange whirring noise. It was barely noticeable above the air circulation pumps.

Maneuvering my wheelchair backward, I hid beside another minidome. I froze and waited.

The whirring noise grew louder.

Seconds later, I discovered what it was.

A robot. The high-tech one I'd seen the day I was outside the dome.

I followed.

I guessed that the newer model robot had video lenses to give it four-directional visuals. And that it could also sense my body heat. So I let it move down the path, well out of sight, before I rolled after it, keeping it in range by listening for the whirring of its motor.

I didn't have to follow far. Partly because the entire dome is a circle only 400 yards in diameter. And partly because the robot stopped almost immediately once it passed all the minidomes and reached the storage areas.

Slowly I rolled to the shadows at the edge of the last minidome and peered around the corner.

The robot stood in front of the locked room that held the Hammerhead. One of its sleek titanium arms reached toward the door handle. The titanium fingers gripped the handle and sheared it off.

I gasped quietly. I could tell this new robot had strength that doubled or tripled my own robot's.

The door swung open.

At this time of night, I knew the robot meant to damage the Hammerhead. But what could I do? If I went to get help, what might the robot do in the few minutes I was gone?

And yet there was no way I could sneak up on it. Not if it had infrared sensors like my own robot.

I leaped to a decision and rolled my wheelchair forward.

The robot must have sensed my body heat. Halfway

across the short space between the storage area and the minidomes, it turned toward me. Even in the dim light, its silver skin gleamed.

"No closer," it said quietly.

I had expected the odd monotone of synthetic vocal cords, like on my robot. But this one sounded very human.

I did not stop.

"Human, you are in peril of your life."

I still did not stop.

"Turn around, human."

I finally did stop, but I didn't turn around. I was only a few feet from the robot. Like mine, it was the height of a full-grown man, so I had to lean my head back to see straight into its forward video lens.

"Leave the Hammerhead alone," I told it, "or I will disable you."

I knew where to disable the robot. Or at least I hoped I knew where. Although it was a second-generation robot, I doubted the power source would be much different than mine—at the back, near the connection to its wheels. A simple tug on a main wire would disconnect the power from the robot's battery pack.

"Go away," it said.

Instead, I closed the short distance between us.

In one swift move, the robot's left hand reached out and grabbed my throat. The titanium fingers tightened slightly, enough to keep me from speaking but not enough to choke me completely. I knew it had the strength to rip my head from my body.

This was my gamble. That I had it figured out right. That only one person under this dome was young enough to have had an operation to let her handle this robot by remote. If I was wrong, the robot hand around my throat would squeeze the life out of me.

"Human, this is your last chance. Blink twice to tell me you will leave."

I blinked twice.

The robot hand dropped from my throat.

I was able to speak again. "I will leave, but only if you agree to meet me at the telescope. In five minutes."

"Not possible, human."

"Knock off this 'human' stuff," I said. "You know my name. Just like I know yours."

Its hand reached for my throat again. I put up my arms, one on each side of my throat, so that its fingers couldn't reach all the way around.

"Listen," I said, "I don't know what your game is. But if you want to stop me from disconnecting your power, you're going to have to kill me. And if you decide not to kill me, meet me at the telescope in five minutes." I continued to stare into the unblinking eye of the video lens.

Finally that large titanium hand with its powerful, deadly fingers dropped.

In an instant, I rolled behind the robot and yanked loose its power cord.

CHAPTER 14

"Hello, Ashley," I said in a reserved tone when I rolled the final few feet onto the platform. "Nice that we could meet."

So it *had* been her handling the robot.

She sat on the bench at the side of the telescope and leaned forward, her elbows on her knees. Shadows hid her face. Above us, through the small, clear-glass bubble, a million stars sprinkled the universe. Below us, the main level of the dome was completely quiet.

"Hello, Tyce. I expected you'd try to talk to me a lot earlier. Like maybe right after we finished the flight-simulator program."

"Like right after I blew your torpedo into tiny bits of space garbage."

"Something like that." Ashley let out a long breath.

"You knew back then, didn't you? When you told me that you were going to try blasting the moon as a way to get the other pilot?"

"No. When I told you that, I was only guessing. I only knew for sure when the other pilot stopped following and waited for Phobos to explode. You're the only person who could have known I was going to try it. Just like you're the only person who knew I was going to try the heat-vent trick the time before. Only in the first combat mission, I still trusted you."

I moved beside her and pointed at a small pack on her back. "The new computer remote?"

She nodded. "Wired into my plug. I can go anywhere with it."

"How handy. I guess I'm using ancient technology. I need to be strapped to a bed." I rolled away from her and stared up at the cold stars.

"How did you figure it out?" Ashley asked.

I didn't answer. I was too sad. Too bitter.

I did, however, have a long list of reasons. A while back, she'd asked if I was ready to go to Jupiter. She was half joking, but how could she have known unless she already knew about the Hammerhead? Then there was the fact that in my first combat mission, the other pilot knew I'd come out of a heat mushroom invisible, with no power. Discovering there was another robot, though, had made me first wonder about her. No one else at the dome could have been young enough for a plug implant. By the time a person is more than five years old, the spine and nervous system have grown too much to make the biological implant work.

"How?" I asked her.

She knew what I meant.

"Dr. Jordan." She stopped, then started again. "I mean, my father. He designed the program. It was no problem for him to access the mainframe computer and plug me into it during the times you were scheduled for flight-simulation combat operations."

"Why? Why keep it a secret?"

"I wish I could tell you why I'm here," Ashley said, "but I can't."

That wasn't the question I was asking. But since she took it that way, I continued. "Why are you practicing in a second-generation robot? Why is it such a secret? Who is forcing you to keep it a secret? We could have been working together every day."

That's what hurt the worst. She'd been here a couple of months. We'd become friends. Great friends. All along she'd let me talk about my robot. When we'd first met, I'd been in the robot body, and she'd pretended not to know how it worked. I wondered how much else of our friendship was a lie.

Tears shimmered in her eyes. "I can't answer any of those questions." She let out another breath.

"Can't? Or won't?"

Ashley hesitated a long time. "Won't."

"I was dumb to think we were friends," I said angrily.

"Tyce, I can't tell you. It would hurt too many others. Even that is saying too much. I don't know how to make you understand that."

I felt so betrayed that I wanted to lash out at her. But I couldn't turn in my wheelchair and swing a fist at her. So I turned my head and used words. "You've talked to me for hours about how important your faith is to you. I guess it's the kind of faith that lets you do whatever you want to other people."

Ashley had once given me one of her silver earrings. In the shape of a cross. It hung around my neck on a thin, silver chain. I lifted it off my neck and held it out. "Take this back," I said. "It doesn't mean anything to me."

I got a gasp of pain from her, and I still didn't stop. "That was cheap, you know, what you did in that first combat mission, setting me up with the heat-vent trick. You could have at least made the combat missions a fair fight."

I threw the silver chain and cross at her. She caught it and stared at it.

"I didn't blow you up in that first combat," Ashley said quietly. "I had a chance but didn't. Remember?"

"All I remember," I said, gritting my teeth, "is that we talked about the heat-vent trick and you used it against me. Let me repeat: I was set up."

"Like you did when you set me up on the second combat mission? Why else tell me you were going to blow up Phobos, then fake it during flight simulation?"

"I only did that," I said, "because I wondered if you were the other pilot. It proved you were. And it proved you are a backstabbing liar."

I heard a muffled sound. It took a second to figure it out.

Ashley was crying. She held her face in her hands and choked back the sobs. Her shoulders heaved. Her words came out in ragged gasps. "I had to win so I'd be the test pilot tomorrow. You didn't know it was a contest, and . . ."

She had to fight for breath, but her tears didn't make me feel sorry for her. Because of one simple thing. What I'd seen only minutes earlier down on the main level.

"When you didn't win, you decided to wreck the Hammerhead so I couldn't fly. That's why you sent your robot there. To spoil what you couldn't have."

Ashley spoke as if she were now gritting her teeth in great pain. "You . . . don't . . . understand. . . ."

"Then make me understand." I said coldly, facing her again.

"I needed to be the pilot. Because I know why they want it tested. And I have to stop them."

"Stop them?" I demanded. "Who? What needs to be stopped?"

"Tyce—"

A voice from below interrupted us. "Ashley? Ashley?"

Dr. Jordan. Her father. Calling softly so the scientists and techies wouldn't be disturbed.

Ashley sat upright, as if she'd been shot. "He can't know we've talked!"

"Make me understand," I said, "or I'll call him up here right now."

She walked the short space between us. Dropping to her knees at the side of my wheelchair, she pleaded, "Please help me. Telling you what I know could cost me my life."

"No," I said. "You made the problem. You deal with it."

His voice drifted up to us again. "Ashley? Ashley?"

She gripped my arm. I pulled it away.

"Tyce, please. Yes, call him up here. But let me get away first so I'll have time to reconnect the power supply to the robot. He can't know I moved it. This is a life-or-death thing."

"Ashley?" her father continued to call. "Ashley?"

She gripped my arm again.

"I think I'll let him keep wandering until he finds the robot," I said. "Unless you have a few things you'd like to tell me."

"There's a simple glitch in the programming of the telescope's computer. You can fix it easily. Only don't let anyone know you've fixed it, because then Dr. Jordan will realize I've told you. Fix it, then look for the comet. If you don't see it, miss your targets tomorrow on the test run. That's why I wanted to be the pilot. Hitting those targets will kill millions on Earth. Believe me. Millions. And they're set up to do that on this mission."

How does she know this? Why didn't she tell me earlier? "Give me one good reason to believe you," I said.

There was a long silence. When Ashley finally spoke again, it was as if someone had pulled a noose tightly around her throat. "Remember I told you I grew up in Denver."

Yes, I remembered. Asking her about the tornado was just one more clue that she'd lied to me.

"I didn't," she whispered. "That's what I'm supposed to tell everyone. Just like I'm supposed to tell everyone that Dr. Jordan is a quantum physicist. He's not. He's an expert in artificial intelligence. And more."

"More?"

Ashley ignored my question. "When I met you, I just wanted to be friends. I should have known from the beginning all of this would happen."

Everything she told me just led to more questions. "I still haven't heard a good reason to believe you," I said.

"Please. Give me a chance to get back down to the main level," she said softly. "Then call him up here. Delay him as long as you can so I can move the robot. There are others. Like us. And we are their only hope."

She placed the silver chain and cross on my lap.

Then she ran.

CHAPTER 15

Dr. Jordan reached the telescope platform five minutes later. He scowled down at me.

I hadn't seen much of him since he'd arrived on the last shuttle. Just glimpses as he hurried from one minidome to another.

His face was round, like his gold-rimmed glasses. His goatee was round too, and his nose was turned up at the end, showing the dark of his nostrils as two more circles.

To me, the strange thing was that Ashley didn't look anything at all like him. Ashley hated talking about her family. All she'd ever said was that her father and mother had divorced. Maybe Ashley looked a lot more like her mother. Or maybe Ashley was even adopted. Whatever it was, it didn't seem like Ashley was able to get along with her father like a friend, which was sad. I was lucky with my parents.

"Is Ashley here?" Dr. Jordan demanded.

I thought it was a dumb question from a scientist who was supposed to be so smart. What did he think—that she was hiding beneath my wheelchair? "I heard you calling for her," I said. "I was just wondering if she was okay."

His impatience with me turned his scowling mouth into a tight little circle. I wondered if he knew that about himself—that his face was a bunch of little circles within a larger circle.

"Unless she stepped out of the dome in the middle of the night, of course she's okay."

"But you're looking for her."

"That's her business and mine."

"Well," I said, "I was just wondering if I could help."

"I doubt it," Dr. Jordan snapped. Then his irritation turned to brief puzzlement. "What are you doing up here, anyway? You should be getting rest. Tomorrow's your real test run in the Hammerhead."

"I couldn't sleep. So I came up here to look at the stars."

"The telescope isn't functioning."

I pointed to the clear glass of the dome above us. "But my eyes work. It's beautiful, isn't it? The Martian night sky."

"Beauty is only something attributed by sentimental humans," he hissed. "Those stars are simply big balls of hydrogen fusing into helium, throwing off light and heat in the process. What you are looking at is physics. Beauty isn't measurable, so it doesn't exist."

"Oh."

"Good night," he said curtly. "Don't waste my time again. And I advise you to get some sleep."

Sleep?

No. If Ashley was right about the telescope, it wouldn't be difficult to find out. The telescope was computer driven, with a small screen and keyboard beside the eyepiece. Viewers keyboarded coordinates or the names of stars, planets, or constellations, and the telescope, when it was working, would track the specified object.

Rawling had long ago given me a password to let me enter the system. I knew the basics of computer programming. I entered the system and did some minor hacking. It took some very simple programming and less than five minutes to make the tracking systems operational again. Then the telescope hummed on its gears as it swung into action.

A half hour later, I was back on the telescope platform with Dad beside me. His face was pressed against the eyepiece. His hair stuck out in all directions, but at four in the morning, a person should not be expected to look his best.

Dad sat back from the eyepiece and turned toward me. "I don't see anything. Where's this great astronomical discovery you promised?"

"My point exactly."

"Tyce, when you woke me up and insisted I come up here, I didn't complain. Sure, I had some questions about why you were out of our minidome at this time of night, but when you refused to answer, I trusted you had a good reason. So here I am. Awake when I should be asleep. And you're telling me your great astronomical discovery is nothing?"

"Yes," I said. "In one way, that's the best news you could get."

"Sure," Dad said, but I knew he didn't mean it. "I'm going back to bed before I get mad. Tomorrow we're going to discuss this. When I'll be awake enough to enjoy being mad at you."

"Listen to me. Don't you find it surprising that the telescope is working again?"

He shrugged. "Not really. I assumed that one of the techies fixed it today."

"No," I said. "I did. Half an hour ago. All it took was some simple rewriting of the computer code."

I wondered why the techies hadn't been able to figure it out. And why Ashley knew about the computer error. But

I'd worry about all of that later. Especially with what I was about to tell Dad.

"So you fixed it." Dad yawned. "Is that such a big deal that you pull me out of bed?"

"If I waited until morning," I said, "you wouldn't have been able to use the telescope during the daylight. I didn't want to wait until tomorrow night to show you."

He snorted. "Might as well use it during the day. Doesn't make much difference if you're not seeing anything spectacular during the night."

"I've got the coordinates of the telescope set up to where the Earth scientists tell us the killer comet is sweeping past Jupiter."

Dad frowned at me, then leaned forward again into the eyepiece of the telescope. He spent 30 seconds squinting. He leaned back. "I don't see it. You sure you have the right coordinates?"

"I triple-checked," I answered.

"But there's no comet."

"And that," I said, "is my big discovery. There is no comet." Some of my trust in Ashley was coming back. If only I could ask her more questions.

"No comet? That doesn't make sense."

"The telescope wasn't working," I said. "Almost as if somebody wanted us to believe there was a comet and didn't want us to be able to check it out for ourselves."

Dad took a quick look through the eyepiece again. He spoke as he stared out into space. "But why would someone want everyone to believe a deadly comet threatened to hit Mars?"

"That," I said, "is a very, very good question."

CHAPTER 16

The next day, I had wanted to wake earlier than I did so I could talk to Ashley. But I hadn't managed to fall asleep until five in the morning.

When I finally woke up, it was like I was coming out of a coma. Usually all Mom or Dad has to do is call my name and I wake up. This time, Dad had to shake my shoulders.

"Huh?" I blinked, trying to focus my eyes.

"Two hours until countdown," he answered. "We wanted to let you sleep as long as possible. But Rawling is here and wants to talk."

I swallowed a few times, trying to get moisture in my mouth. I remembered last night's events. "Does he know about the comet?"

Dad nodded. "That's why he's here."

"I'll be right out."

Minutes later I rolled into the common area of our minidome.

Rawling had a cup of coffee in his hand. He smiled bleakly at me. "We don't have much time. I wish I could call off this test run, but I can't. It would go against direct orders from Earth. So we need to talk about a comet that doesn't exist. And about a Hammerhead that does exist but gets shipped here in secrecy. Whatever we talk about, we keep quiet until we figure this out." Sipping his coffee, he made a face. He always complained that he missed Earth coffee more than anything else.

"There's more," I said.

Rawling lifted his eyebrow.

"Ashley. She's the one who handles the other robot."

He set his coffee down, an intense look on his face. "I'd thought the same but had no way of proving it. She's the only other person under the dome young enough to have the bio-implant. How did you find out?"

I told him about my conversation with her last night.

"Let me get this straight," Rawling said. "Both times you were in the flight-simulation combat, she was the other pilot?"

Dad poured more coffee into his cup and offered a refill to Rawling.

Rawling took it, sipped, and grimaced again.

"All I can think of," I said, "is that she works with Dr. Jordan the same way I work with you. It wouldn't be difficult for Dr. Jordan to know when you had me scheduled for the flight simulations. All he'd need to do is get into the computer mainframe and link Ashley into it the same way that I do. I mean, the flight simulation is basically a virtual-reality computer game. In a computer game, you can play the computer or a human opponent, right? Dr. Jordan just needed to get Ashley into the game."

"Sure," Rawling said. "But if that's the case, why wouldn't Dr. Jordan let us know that Ashley was part of this? That's what is driving me crazy. All the secrets here."

"Not just secrets here," Dad corrected, "but secrets from Earth. Let's face it. Someone there is making the decisions to spend the money they did on the Hammerhead. Someone there was able to fake the shipment papers. Someone there sent us the communications about a killer comet. We've been thrown into a game where we don't know the rules."

"We've been thrown into a game without being told the game is happening," Rawling said. "And the biggest question of all is why."

They had begun to talk to each other like I wasn't there. I had to cough to get their attention. They turned to me.

"I've got a guess," I said. "At least a guess about the reason for the comet and the Hammerhead."

I told them. Then I told them when and where I wanted to ask the questions I had about my guess.

I couldn't find Ashley in the last hour before we went into the countdown preparations. I discovered why when I finally gave up looking and wheeled over to the platform buggy that would take us out to the launch site, about two miles from the dome.

Ashley was there. Inside the buggy. With Dad and Dr. Jordan. She wouldn't meet my eyes.

Dr. Jordan did, though. "Ashley's here to observe," he said to my unspoken question. "Today's an exciting day in space history. I want her to be part of it."

Ashley didn't look excited. I thought I knew why. But only the next few hours would let me know if I was right.

CHAPTER 17

The launch was routine, or at least as routine as you could expect anytime 500,000 horsepower was generated to break several tons of equipment and rocket fuel away from the gravity and atmosphere of a planet.

I wasn't worried anyway.

My dad was the best. He'd shuttled the Habitat Lander between the surface of Mars and the orbiting Crew Transfer Vehicle dozens of times. That was how interplanetary travel worked. The CTV was large and comfortable enough for the eight-month journey to Earth. In space, with no air friction or gravity, it didn't matter whether a vehicle weighed 2 tons or 10. If I'd been able to brace against something, a simple push of my arm would be enough to send the CTV on its way.

But launching a CTV from planetary gravity was a

totally different story. It would take megatons of fuel and demand an aerodynamic construction like a rocket ship, limiting the room for crew. So the CTV instead orbited Mars, and the Habitat Lander was used to carry things back and forth from Mars (or Earth, if the CTV was parked there).

The Habitat Lander was much smaller. With Dad as pilot, Dr. Jordan, Ashley, and me—all of us strapped in against the g-forces on takeoff and landing—there was barely enough room for the extra space suits. The Hammerhead had been secured in the cargo bay.

No one said much before takeoff. We were all in space suits, but that wasn't the reason for silence. Space suits are connected by radio, and we could have heard each other easily.

Dad was looking down at his countdown checklist.

Dr. Jordan still looked angry. I'd overheard him yelling at Rawling this morning. He'd been furious that someone had broken the lock to the storage room. I'd seen him check out the Hammerhead at least a dozen times after that, probably making sure it hadn't been tampered with.

Ashley seemed unusually quiet. I hadn't spoken with her since last night, when we'd been at the telescope. Now she wouldn't even make eye contact with me. I hadn't had a chance to tell her that I hadn't ratted her out. Instead, I'd calmly invited Dr. Jordan to look at the stars with me when he made it up to the telescope. I hadn't had a chance to tell her that he had hissed impatiently at me. And then he stomped away, complaining about wasted time.

I didn't have much to say. At least not yet. I was angry too, but for a very different reason.

Just then the rockets roared. The Habitat Lander shook hard, as if Mars were a giant dog reluctant to let it go. A minute later we broke from the planet and shot through the air. G-forces flattened my face.

This was my first trip into space. I should have been enjoying it. I should have been excited about getting into orbit and seeing Mars for the first time the way I'd been seeing it in the virtual-reality computer programs.

But I didn't enjoy the trip. Like Ashley, I'd lost a lot of my excitement.

CHAPTER 18

Once we were in orbit, getting into the Hammerhead was
relatively simple.

I was already in my space suit. That part had been
awkward on Mars because of the low gravity. Dad had helped
push my legs inside.

Here in orbit, however, it didn't matter that I couldn't
use my legs. Moving was as easy as pushing off with a
finger or elbow. Any other time I would have loved that
freedom. But I had to focus on what I needed to do, so
I didn't even look out through the observatory windows
at Mars.

"Right behind you, Tyce," Dad said into his space suit
radio when I reached the sealed doors that led to the cargo
bay. "Remember the space pilot's first rule. If for any reason

you think it's unsafe to proceed, you can abort the flight. This isn't about trying to be brave."

"Roger," I said, knowing Ashley and Dr. Jordan were on the same channel.

The cargo bay doors worked on the same principle as the entrance to the dome. When the inner door opened, some of the air from the ship filled the cargo bay. You stepped inside, and the inner door closed before the outer door opened.

Dad had explained to me earlier that when that outer door opened, the vacuum of outer space sucked smaller, unsecured contents out through the gap like a miniature explosion. Humans in space suits were flexible enough to get sucked out in the first surge. So he had warned me to buckle the safety cable of my space suit to the iron rings set inside the cargo bay. If I tumbled out, I'd go with so much speed that the chances of any space vehicle finding me out in space were next to zero. I'd be doomed to a slow death, floating in space as I waited for my oxygen and water to run out.

Dad floated behind me as I punched the button to open the inner cargo door. We'd worked it out beforehand. He would enter the cargo bay with me and help me into the Hammerhead. Once I was secured inside the space torpedo, he would reenter the Habitat Lander, close the inner door again, and finally open the outer door to set the Hammerhead free. He, Dr. Jordan, and Ashley would be able to watch from the observatory window.

Out here in space, time seemed not to exist. Our slow, weightless movements felt eerie.

We waited until the inner door slid open, and Dad followed me into the cargo bay.

"Safety clip," Dad said, pointing at the iron rings. I started to buckle my safety cable in place, and so did he.

"Roger." Someday I was going to ask Dad or Rawling where that phrase came from. Meanwhile, it sounded cool so I used it.

Dad fumbled with the catch of the Hammerhead's hatch.

When it finally opened, I pulled myself inside. It was a tight fit, space suit and all.

Once I was inside, with the hatch still open, Dad unclipped my safety cable. The end of it retracted, following me into the Hammerhead.

"Everything still fine, Son?"

"Roger."

Dad secured the hatch. "I'm not leaving the cargo area until you hook yourself up to the onboard computer. Remember the space pilot's first rule. If for any reason—"

I grinned and finished his words. "—I think it's unsafe to proceed, I have the right to abort the flight."

It took me five minutes to get the onboard computer ready. My plug had already been attached to an antenna wired into my space suit. It traded signals with the Hammerhead's onboard computer, and when they had finished talking to each other, everything was ready.

There was a small observatory port in the Hammerhead. I lifted an arm to give Dad a thumbs-up.

He saw it and nodded. "Run through your checklist with me."

I did.

"You're ready," Dad said. "The Hammerhead is hooked by a safety cable to the inside of this cargo bay. When the outer door opens, you get pulled out 20 or 30 yards. I will repeat that the pilot—you—has the control switch to release that safety cable. In other words, the flight is your decision. Because remember the first rule of space pilot safety. If for any reason—"

"I'm fine."

He rapped on the observation panel of the Hammerhead. "I'm proud of you. I love you." With those words, he pushed away.

Thirty seconds later, with the inner door sealed and Dad safely inside the Habitat Lander, the outer cargo door slid open. The Hammerhead bumped against the opening doors as the explosion of pressure shot through the gap. As the doors opened fully, it bobbed out of the cargo bay completely. It stopped at the end of the cable.

The Habitat Lander loomed large in my observation window. I could see Dad and Dr. Jordan at the window.

All that held me to the safety of the orbiting Habitat Lander was a thin, steel cable. When I released it, I would be all alone in space.

I shivered.

CHAPTER 19

Incredible.

I floated in total, peaceful silence. By turning my head, I saw the edge of Mars. It was so large against the black backdrop of space that all I could see was a small part of the red planet's curve and its shimmering atmosphere. In the distance were rings of craters and lines of mountain ranges. When I lifted my eyes, I could see beyond the curve to where a bright blue ball, swirled with white, hung motionless. Earth.

Tears filled my eyes at this beauty.

I wondered if heaven would be anything like this. Total peace. A sense of total freedom. And an overwhelming sense of awe of the God who created all of this.

"Tyce—" Dr. Jordan's brisk voice broke into my

thoughts—"you haven't begun countdown. Do you have any questions before you begin?"

All I had to do was instruct the onboard computer to begin the preignition countdown. Once the rocket flares ignited, the Hammerhead would be mine, responding instantly to my thoughts. I'd be able to race through space. I'd be able to explore a million miles as easily as rolling my wheelchair along a path. I'd be able to flit among the moons of Mars, cruise above the planet, head for the asteroids. But I had questions.

"Yes?" Dr. Jordan sounded impatient.

"I do have several questions, sir."

"Please make them brief. You are familiar with all the controls. The Hammerhead is fully prepared and ready."

"Yes, sir."

I looked at Earth again. Thought of all the lives on that planet. Thought of mothers, fathers, and their kids. Wondered what it would be like to be destroyed in a single burst of red from a space torpedo that circled the Earth.

"Tyce! Your questions?" Dr. Jordan's irritated voice rang in my helmet.

"Sir, this laser that I'm going to use on an asteroid. It has a range of 3,000 miles, correct?"

"Yes, we've been through that. Fire from extreme range to ensure you do not endanger the Hammerhead with asteroid fragments. It is a prototype, worth approximately 15 billion dollars."

"No one has tested this weapon before, sir?"

"Of course not. Which is why you are going on this mission today." Dr. Jordan didn't bother to disguise his sigh at my stupidity.

"But, sir, wouldn't a test like this break all of the non-testing treaties set up by the United Nations? I mean, hasn't there been a ban on any new weapons testing since 2020?"

"Tyce, a comet is two months away from destroying Mars. In these circumstances, today is not a weapons test. It is preparation for the prevention of catastrophe."

Every time I said the word *sir*, I bit it off. Cold and short. Because I was getting angrier and angrier at what it seemed Dr. Jordan really wanted me to do. And it didn't involve a comet. It was something much, much worse.

"I hope you are finished with these pointless questions."

"Almost, sir."

Another one of his aggravated sighs echoed in my helmet.

I kept my eyes on Earth, 50 million miles away—where all those people were unaware of this tiny Hammerhead space torpedo. "Sir, this laser weapon is capable of penetrating a planet's atmosphere," I said.

"Pointless, pointless, pointless," Dr. Jordan muttered.

"Is it, sir? What if I uncabled the Hammerhead and decided to circle Mars and destroy the dome? Is that possible?"

"Your family and friends live beneath that dome. You would not be so insane."

"Sir," I repeated, "does this space torpedo have the capacity to destroy planetary targets?"

There was a long pause. Finally he answered. "In theory, yes, it does."

"Including targets on Earth."

"A ridiculous statement."

"Sir, does this space torpedo have the capacity to destroy targets on Earth?" My eyes could trace the safety cable. It was barely visible—and my only link to the Habitat Lander.

"In theory, yes," he answered. "But your questions are impertinent. If you don't learn to listen better, you probably won't be given a chance to explore space again."

That was a threat, and I understood it very well. But this was more important than my career as a space pilot. "Yes, sir," I said. "I'm afraid I have just a few more questions." The questions that Dad and I and Rawling had discussed in the morning over coffee.

"No," he said, his voice rising. "Begin the countdown."

I gulped and continued. "The earliest any astronomer could have spotted the comet was five months ago. Yet this space torpedo was loaded for shuttle to Mars well before that. Can you explain why?"

Dr. Jordan answered immediately. "If you had any brains, you'd realize design work on the Hammerhead would have begun at least 10 years earlier. Obviously then no one knew the comet would appear. So the conclusion is simple.

This project was started in anticipation that a comet or aster-oid might someday threaten Mars or Earth. It is a timely coincidence that the Hammerhead arrived here when it did."

"A *coincidence*?"

He evidently caught my tone of disbelief. "Do not for-get that, in many ways, the dome is a *military* operation. Insubordination is not an option. Now begin the countdown!"

"Two more questions, sir," I insisted. "One, why is the virtual-reality program set up for pilot combat—if, as you say, the Hammerhead is designed to only fight comets?"

"Begin the countdown!"

"Sir, I believe," I continued stubbornly, "that the Hammerhead is designed as a weapon of war. I believe it will break the weapons ban treaty to test this new laser. I believe once the Hammerhead has proven itself, the military will have the ultimate fighting weapon. And with political unrest on Earth, it will give total dominion to whichever government controls the Hammerhead."

"You are out of line!" Dr. Jordan shouted so loudly that my ears hurt.

My dad interrupted. "Jordan, talk to my son civilly. Or speak to me directly."

"Your *son*." It sounded like Dr. Jordan could hardly hold his anger. "Your *son* is out of order."

"Is he?" Dad asked. "Or is he getting close to the truth here?"

Silence.

I filled it. "Sir, I have just one more question."

If I was right, the Hammerhead would truly be unstoppable. It could circle the Earth at speeds unknown to any previous military weapon. With a red burst, it could hit any target, raining horror down from the sky. I was ready for my final question.

"Dr. Jordan, will you please tell me why the telescope was not operational? Why, when it was fixed, I could not find the comet at the coordinates given to Dr. McTigre?"

Rawling is going to find out more about the techie responsible for the telescope. It can't be an accident—the fact that the telescope wasn't working.

"Mr. Sanders." Dr. Jordan's voice was so furious that it cracked. "Command your son to obey!"

Dad's words came through loud and clear in my helmet. "My son is the pilot. He is in control of the ship. I will respect his decision. As shall you. And I, too, find it very interesting that the comet you say we're targeting does not exist."

I wanted to cheer at the stern anger in Dad's voice.

"Begin the countdown," Dr. Jordan ordered me. *"Immediately."*

"Are you saying that you have no answer?" I asked. "Or are you saying that the threat of a comet does not exist? Are you saying it's a manufactured excuse so that governments on Earth will not question you as you break the international weapons ban treaty to test the greatest military equipment invented in the history of humankind?"

"Begin the countdown. *Immediately*." Dr. Jordan was almost shouting.

"Will you answer my questions?"

"I repeat, begin the countdown!" he yelled full force into my helmet.

"Sir," I said calmly, "might I remind you of the space pilot's first rule?"

"Begin the countdown. Immediately. That is a direct order," Dr. Jordan barked.

He didn't sound like a scientist. He sounded like a military general. My hunch had been proven right.

"Sir, I believe it is unsafe to proceed," I said. "I abort this flight."

CHAPTER 20

Fifteen minutes later, I was inside the Habitat Lander. Part of me ached with regret for how badly I had wanted to take the Hammerhead into space. Yet I knew a few moments of freedom outside my wheelchair compared so little to the terror that the Hammerhead could inflict on Earth, if it was transported back and launched from the moon.

One look at Dr. Jordan's face through his space helmet, and I knew he was furious. His face was puffed with anger. All that showed through his space helmet were his eyes, his nose, and his bared teeth.

He and I both knew he could not force me to fly. No one, not even the highest military general, had the power to make a pilot break the safety rule.

I thought then that I'd won. That even with an hour

until our shuttle finished its orbit and was in position to return to Mars, the Hammerhead would not fly.

I was wrong.

"Ashley," Dr. Jordan said a few seconds after I had pushed my way into the crew area, "remember when I told these two you were merely a sightseer, along for the ride?"

"Yes." Her voice was barely audible in our space helmets.

"Now is the time they learn the truth about you. That you, too, are capable as a test pilot."

Ashley nodded very slowly. A glint of silver inside her space visor caught my eye from the earring she wore. The one that matched mine around my neck. Seeing the earring reassured me. I knew what she believed. I could trust her. It was a symbol, too, of our friendship. She wouldn't fly. Not after our conversation on the telescope platform last night.

"Prepare for a target mission," Dr. Jordan hissed.

"Yes," she said.

She's betraying me again! "Ashley! You can't."

"I can. And I will." She paused. "I don't want any help in the cargo bay. Not from either of you."

Now it was reversed. Me in the observation window of the Habitat Lander. Me looking down on the space helmet that showed through the much smaller observation window of the Hammerhead.

The space torpedo was still tethered to the much larger Habitat Lander. It hung in orbit with us. As a backdrop, the giant red surface of Mars moved slowly beneath it.

It could have been me there, ready to explore the space beyond Mars.

But it was Ashley.

And, unlike me, she had begun the preignition countdown.

Tiny flares, each as bright as a sun, suddenly burst from the rocket nozzles of the Hammerhead.

"Excellent, Ashley," Dr. Jordan said. "Now go ahead and release the safety cable."

I could only imagine a click as the Hammerhead released it. The cable floated harmlessly away.

"Thank you, Ashley. You know your mission. Stay in radio contact as long as possible. We will monitor you on radar and with satellite transmitters."

Inside the Hammerhead was the equivalent of a GPS, which would fire radio waves back to a locator on the Habitat Lander.

"Yes," Ashley said. "But I won't make it past Phobos."

"I don't understand," Dr. Jordan said.

"Watch," she replied. "You'll understand soon enough."

The Hammerhead lifted slightly and hovered beside the

Habitat Lander's observation window. Through the small window of the Hammerhead, I couldn't see Ashley's face—just the dark globe of her space helmet against the lighter background of her space suit.

"Tyce," Ashley said. "Good-bye, my friend. I wish it didn't have to be like this. I wish it could have been different. Remember what I told you at the telescope. Remember the silver earring."

Then the Hammerhead waggled, like fingers waving good-bye.

With a burst of brightness, she and the Hammerhead disappeared into the solar system.

We watched it on radar. For 3,500 miles the Hammerhead continued to gain speed on its approach to Phobos, that small moon only 18 miles wide.

The Hammerhead did not swerve.

Twenty seconds before impact, Dr. Jordan began to shout in disbelief.

Ten seconds before impact, I began to pray—with my eyes open. I couldn't pull my eyes away from the radar screen, which showed a tiny, fast blip moving toward a bigger, much slower blip.

Five seconds before impact, I moved to the observation window and stared out into the deep black of the solar system.

One second before impact I took a deep breath and said good-bye. By then there was no mistaking Ashley's intent.

It takes bulletlike accuracy to hit the only object in space between Mars and the asteroid belt millions of miles away.

Then there was impact.

I heard it through the alarm bell on the radar screen. And saw it. A bright bloom of light flashed off as quickly as it had flashed on, leaving only the deep darkness of space.

And a deep emptiness in my heart.

CHAPTER 21

Two days had passed since Ashley chose to pilot the Hammerhead into Phobos. For those two days, after arriving back on
Mars, I'd been locked in my room, refusing to talk to anyone
except Mom and Dad.

I knew everyone under the dome would be in shock, and
I didn't want to hear them talk about Ashley being dead. Last
night Mom and Dad told me that the new impact bowl on the
face of Phobos, easily seen from the dome's telescope, had
been named Ashley's Crater. I'm not sure I'll ever want to go
up to the dome's telescope again.

I wonder if anyone on Earth will ever know the
price Ashley paid to keep their blue sky a place of safety,
not death.

After the "test run," I had arrived home so exhausted

that I hadn't even had the strength to put any of my thoughts on my computer. Until now.

It's like what Dad and I just talked about. Every sword always has two edges: a good side and a dangerous side.

Nuclear fission could be used as a source of cheap energy. Or it could make a bomb that would destroy entire cities.

Genetic research could save lives with medical advances. Or be used to create hideous new creatures.

The Hammerhead could help us by sweeping away asteroids or comets that threaten human life. Or it could destroy millions of lives if military people used it to try to control the universe.

And so on. Every new invention or advance could be used for good. Or not for good. That was the two-edged sword.

I leaned back in my wheelchair and sighed.

I wished badly that Ashley would step through the doorway and give me a big grin.

I wished badly that she was up at the telescope, waiting for me.

I wished badly that I could have the chance to apologize for what I'd said to her the other night. I wished I could tell her that I understood she really lived what she believed. That by sacrificing her life, she had given all she could for others.

Most of all, I wished I could go back in time and let her wreck the Hammerhead with her robot, so she wouldn't have had to do it the way she did in space.

But I wouldn't have that chance.

All I'd have were memories.

As Dad explained, evil is part of the two-edged sword. Evil exists because God allows us to make choices. He wants us to *choose* to love and obey him, instead of being forced to do what he wants us to do. As humans, sometimes we choose to do good. But other times we choose to do evil. That's why evil exists, and sometimes bad things happen that are outside our control. Like the fact that Ashley felt she had no other choice than to take the Hammerhead into a direct collision course with Phobos. Otherwise, the Hammerhead could have been used to destroy millions on Earth. And like the fact that she had to be so secretive about her past, in order to protect the others she'd talked about. Just who were those others? I wondered.

Then Dad and I talked about Ashley's death. I asked him why she had to die so young. Dad said he didn't have an answer for that. And that there were some things we would not know until we got to heaven and could ask God face-to-face. The most important thing, Dad said, was to trust in God. To know you had a place in heaven. That you didn't have to be afraid of the mysteries of his universe.

Or think that you should be able to solve them all.

CHAPTER 22

After I finished writing in my journal, I found Dad in the quiet common area of our minidome.

I rolled my wheelchair up to where he sat, drinking coffee and staring at nothing in the darkness.

"You couldn't sleep either, huh?"

"No," I answered.

We sat together for a while, neither of us speaking. I had too many thoughts in my head. I didn't know where to begin.

"I wish I didn't have to go," he said. "I'm going to miss you."

In a few days he'd be leaving again, on another shuttle run to Earth. And taking Blaine Steven and Dr. Jordan with him. Now that Rawling knew Dr. Jordan had been sent here for a weapons test, he'd ordered him deported to Earth.

"I'm going to miss you, Dad. A lot."

More silence.

He put his hand on my shoulder.

"In my thoughts, I keep hearing some of the last things Ashley ever said to me."

Dad waited.

I heard her words clearly up on the telescope platform, the night before the Hammerhead's test mission: *"Tyce, I can't tell you. It would hurt too many others. Even that is saying too much."*

"There was a lot about her we didn't know," I said.

Ashley's words rang in my head: *"Please help me. Telling you what I know could cost me my life."*

I had not helped her. I had not trusted her. And that made me incredibly sad. I owed her more than that, even if she wasn't here. It had taken her life to make me want to help.

"Remember I told you I grew up in Denver. I didn't. That's what I'm supposed to tell everyone."

"Would you help me, Dad?"

"Yes," he said. "With what?"

In the darkness, I blinked back tears. Dad hadn't asked me first with what. He'd simply said yes. He trusted me.

"There are others. Like us. And we are their only hope."

"I want to find out about Ashley. Where she came from. Who she really is. When you get back to Earth, can you do what you can and send e-mails?"

Dad squeezed my shoulder. "I'll do everything I can. You have my promise."

"Thanks."

"There are others. Like us. And we are their only hope."

I didn't know who they were. Or where they were. Or what they needed to give them hope. But Ashley was gone.

That left me.

CHAPTER 23

I didn't sleep well that night.

Dreams I couldn't remember kept waking me up.

I sat up once, calling Ashley's name into the darkness. Then it came back to me what she'd done. I cried into my pillow for a long time.

In the morning, I didn't want to get out of bed. Getting dressed and getting into my wheelchair would mean that the day had started. And when the day started, I'd have to admit to myself that Ashley was gone.

Except, when I finally pulled myself into sitting position, something shiny caught my eye on the seat of my wheelchair.

It was tiny and silver. In the shape of a cross.

An earring. Like the one on a silver chain around my neck.

I felt for mine, wondering if it had somehow fallen off.

It hadn't. It was still there. With the matching one on the seat of my wheelchair. As if someone had placed it there while I slept.

Ashley?

SCIENCE AND GOD

You've probably noticed that the question of God's existence comes up in Robot Wars.

It's no accident, of course. I think this is one of the most important questions that we need to decide for ourselves. If God created the universe and there is more to life than what we can see, hear, taste, smell, or touch, that means we have to think of our own lives as more than just the time we spend on Earth.

On the other hand, if this universe was not created and God does not exist, then that might really change how you view your existence and how you live.

Sometimes science is presented in such a way that it suggests there is no God. To make any decision, it helps to know as much about the situation as possible. As you decide for yourself, I'd like to show in the Robot Wars series that many, many people—including famous scientists—don't see science this way.

As you might guess, I've spent a lot of time wondering about science and God, and I've spent a lot of time reading about what scientists have learned and concluded. Because of this, I wrote a nonfiction book called *Who Made The Moon?* and you can find information about it at www.whomadethemoon.com. If you ever read it, you'll see why science does not need to keep anyone away from God.

With that in mind, I've added a little bit more to this book—a couple of essays about the science in journals one and two of Robot Wars, based on what you can find in *Who Made The Moon?*

Sigmund Brouwer
www.whomadethemoon.com

CAN WE EXPECT SCIENCE TO BE OUR SAVIOR?

Q: What's ahead?

A: For the first 10,000 years of recorded human history, the fastest that any human could travel was the speed of a galloping horse. (Unless someone wanted to jump off a building or a cliff!) Horse-drawn wagons were very slow, wind-powered ships were slow, the first trains were slow, and even the first automobiles were slow.

It's only in the last hundred years or so—the tiniest sliver of time—that technology has allowed us to travel faster. Some cars go as fast as 200 miles an hour. Airplanes can go faster than sound. A journey that took the early American settlers weeks or months by wagon over dangerous territory, we can accomplish in hours on an interstate in air-conditioned comfort.

In fact, thanks to science and technology, most of us truly live better than kings did only 100 years ago. We live in heated homes with running water, HDTVs, and washers and dryers. Doctors no longer try to cure us by applying leeches to our heads to suck blood; we can get the best of modern drugs and operations. We're protected by electronic security systems and police forces; we probably don't lie awake at night worrying about barbarians tearing down our town. We store our wealth in electronic binary codes in bank computers, not in piles of gold or silver that armies can steal.

And these improvements in science and technology are happening faster and faster. After all, it was only 40 years ago that a man first stepped on the moon.

Now SUVs have more technology than the first spaceships, and your computer has more calculating power than the computers that placed the first men on the moon. With cell phones and computers, you can instantly communicate through satellites to locations anywhere in the world.

Medicine? Your body can be vaccinated, wired, and soon, cloned.

Even color TVs aren't very old. Now you can entertain yourself with the virtual reality of music videos, computer games, and theater screens three stories tall.

Science and technology are staggering, amazing, incredible. Who knows how many more leaps ahead we will be by AD 2039, the date of this story? And what's even more exciting is that you, like Tyce Sanders and his virtual-reality missions, may be the one who helps discover this new technology!

Q: Can science and technology stop crime? Can they prevent heartache, loneliness, fear? Can they make families perfect? Can they prevent death?

A: The answer to all of the questions is obvious. No.

Although the conditions around you have improved with blinding speed, you can still suffer pain, guilt, heartache, fear, and loneliness deep inside you. Where it matters.

Those who look to science and technology to save us as a human race assume we just don't know enough yet. But learning more about our world and how it works doesn't make problems go away. The answer is all too obvious. All you need to do is read the headlines of a newspaper or watch the daily news to see it.

The real problem—sadly—is the choices we make. Some are good choices. Others are hurtful, evil choices. Because God loves us, he gives us the power to choose. But then we have to live with the consequences.

The bottom line is that science and technology are incredible tools for exploring what it means to be human— and for helping other humans, if used properly. But science and technology cannot change anyone's heart. And they'll never give meaning or hope or peace to your life.

JOURNAL TWO
WHY DO BAD
THINGS HAPPEN?

Q: Why does God allow bad things to happen to people he says he loves?

A: This is one of the most difficult questions every person asks sometime in his or her life. And what you believe about the answer is really important. Why? Because if you decide that God allows bad things to happen because he's weak and can't stop them or because he doesn't care about us after all, then you won't really want to believe in God. You'll come to think that he doesn't exist—except as a character in Bible stories.

Part of why evil exists is because God allows all of us the freedom to make choices—to do good things or bad things. When you choose to do good things, the world is a much better place. When you choose to do bad things, you hurt others—and yourself in the long run.

Other people are also making good and bad choices. That's why you'll hear all sorts of bad things happening in the news. (There are lots of good things happening too, but those events hardly ever make the news.)

Q: Do bad things or the news of bad things mean that God doesn't care?
A: Since the beginning of the history of writing, hundreds of books have tried to answer this difficult question.

Perhaps the best and most famous book on the subject is found in the Bible—the book of Job. Job loved God, and he was also rich. Then one day, through no fault of his own, he lost his possessions, his children, and his health. No wonder he asked why God allowed suffering.

His friends mistakenly told Job it was because of things he'd done wrong. But Job, through asking questions, learned important things.

He learned that, while suffering might be a consequence of wrong choices, bad things do happen to good people, just as sometimes good things happen to bad people. You can't always control what happens to you, but you can control how you choose to deal with what happens.

Job learned that God was always close to him, even when God might seem far away. This matters a great deal, because we need to believe in God for *who he is*, not what we want him to be. Some people think of God as a Santa or a genie who gives them what they want. But God is really the awesome Creator of the universe who sees the beginning and end of all things. He isn't limited by seeing only this time. And that's why God won't always explain everything to us. There are mysteries we'll never understand while we're on Earth.

What's the greatest thing Job learned? That even when everything was taken away, he could still trust God. Why? Because God is all we have and need. That truth is both sad and hopeful. It's sad, because someday death will take each of us away from our possessions and our health and our loved ones. But sad as death is, we have an incredible hope. We know that life on Earth, with all its pain, is not our final destination.

No matter what happens around you, you can trust God. Nothing can separate you from his love.

ABOUT THE AUTHOR

Sigmund Brouwer and his wife, recording artist Cindy
Morgan, and their daughters split living between Red Deer,
Alberta, Canada, and Nashville, Tennessee. He has written
several series of juvenile fiction and eight novels. Sigmund
loves sports and plays golf and hockey. He also enjoys visiting
schools to talk about books. He welcomes visitors to his Web
site at www.coolreading.com.